TWILIGHT

Joey had the feeling that a powerful drug had taken control of his senses. His limbs seemed to float free of his body and his impressions were distorted and confused. For some reason he remembered something that had happened years ago when they'd lived in Florida. Fishing in a friend's rowboat, Joey'd jumped in to do some snorkeling and had seen a barracuda. It had hovered, silent and motionless, in the water, watching Joey with its hard, flat eye and Joey had known right then who was master in those waters and who had better get out while there was still time.

With a gigantic effort, Joey dragged himself to his feet, forcing his thoughts away from this long-ago encounter and extended a hand to the approaching Mr. Wynn.

"Prescott, isn't it?" asked the man in a deep, resonant voice. "I hear you did pretty well in today's scrimmage."

"It was a good day, sir," answered Joey. He was surprised to hear his voice so calm. *Now what came over me?* he asked himself. *What just happened?*

Play to Live

CHARLES VELEY

TWILIGHT

WHERE DARKNESS BEGINS...

Published by
Dell Publishing Co., Inc.
1 Dag Hammarskjold Plaza
New York, N.Y. 10017

Laurel-Leaf Library ® TM 766734,
Dell Publishing Co., Inc.

Twilight™ is a trademark of
Dell Publishing Co., Inc., New York, New York.

ISBN: 0-440-96950-6
RL:6.4
Printed in the United States of America

First printing—December 1982

Chapter One

It was dark when Joey awoke. Rain dripped steadily off the roof and splashed onto the edge of the wooden floorboards of the bunkhouse. For a moment Joey didn't know where he was. Then he remembered. Football camp. Raising himself on one elbow and looking around, he could just make out the huddled forms of the others in their bunks. Shivering, Joey drew his blanket around his shoulders. Summer was near its end in these isolated mountains.

The luminous dial of his watch read 4:32 A.M. What was he doing awake at this hour? Usually he slept right up until the coach's whistle blew at five. It must have been the cold that woke him, Joey thought.

Pushing aside the cold canvas flap of the bunkhouse, Joey peered into the dark and fog outside. Nothing. He was about to close the flap when a noise made him stop. Was that a car's engine? Joey strained to see. There. By the other bunkhouse, glowing like red eyes ... those were a car's brake lights, weren't they? A gust of wind spattered rain in his face and he turned his head. When he looked again the lights were gone.

The wind rattled the canvas flap. Joey's mattress and blanket were getting soaked. *Forget it,* he thought. *Just a car. Go back to sleep.* But he couldn't, knowing that in less than half an hour he and the other boys would be groping for their pads, pulling on damp, cold uniforms, stumbling out to the muddy practice field for calisthenics.

Lying back on his bunk, Joey began to go over the events of the past few weeks. Once again he was the new kid in town, even though this was his senior year of high school. "You'll make lots of new friends," his parents always told him each time they'd moved. And he had. Dark-haired and lean, with his mother's sensitive features and his father's gift for Irish blarney, Joey had always made friends easily. Then came the time when he had to say good-bye and move on. . . .

But his parents had high hopes for Norwich, their new home. Joey would be needing a scholarship for college next year, and Norwich was favored to win its seventh straight championship this season. College recruiters would be flocking to the games and would see Joey play. The way his father saw things, it was only a matter of weeks until the big-name coaches would be stuffing his mailbox with invitations to visit their campuses.

If Joey played. *If* he made the starting team. Right now, that was a big "if."

It was true, Joey admitted to himself, he was on the edge. At the other schools he'd always been *sure* he'd play first-string, and he always had. Just a shade under six feet tall, wiry and quick, his muscles hardened from regular workouts, Joey had always been as fast as the other team members, hit just as hard, picked up the plays just as quickly. . . . Here he'd been fumbling. Where had his confidence gone? What made him *feel* so different since they'd moved to Norwich?

Everything in Norwich was different. When you first drove over the mountains and saw the cluster of buildings beside the winding river, Norwich looked picturesque and quaint. But when you drove down the main street you saw the dingy old buildings with cracked plastic signs and the cinders spread over last year's snow still in dirty gray piles along the curbs. The only new store in town was Wynn's Sporting Goods, which occupied nearly a full block and had its own three-story parking garage. Joey hadn't been in there yet; the Prescotts had been in Norwich for only three weeks and they weren't going to splurge on much of anything except the necessities until his father got his first paycheck —

Joey sighed. Money problems, the scholarship on the line, last chance to make good ... he really felt under the gun. Certainly other kids at this camp for pre-season practice seemed to feel under pressure as well. When they pulled their helmets on each morning they were grim-faced, like combat troopers heading out to battle with the enemy.

Joey had never seen this kind of intensity before. The guys all thought that making the Norwich starting team was the be-all and end-all of existence. Once a starter, you were "set for life," according to Andy Blair, who lived next door to the house Joey's parents had rented. Also a senior, Andy was desperate to make the starting lineup; it was his last chance. He whispered wild tales to Joey of the rewards that awaited Norwich varsity players: pool tables in their basements, big-screen Betamax sets in their living rooms ...

But in the next bunk, Andy slept peacefully. Joey turned over and propped his chin in his hands. *I can't let the pressure get to me,* he told himself.

On the practice field an hour later it was still raining. They had gone through stretches and quick cals and were working on agility drills when Joey noticed a silver-gray Mercedes-Benz appear out of the mist at the edge of the woods.

Moving slowly, the sedan splashed through the ruts that bordered the grass. Fog billowed from its exhaust pipe as it circled the field. The car stopped about twenty yards from the group, its motor running and the windshield wipers sweeping raindrops from the glass.

Joey was certain that this was the car he'd heard that morning. He didn't know why, but he was sure. He was sure, too, the car was watching *him*.

The others seemed to recognize the car. Faces went rigid; eyes hardened with determination. The coach's whistle shrilled and the pace of the workout quickened.

Grit and mud chafed Joey's neck beneath his shoulder pads as he hit the ground, rolled, and came up running in place.

"Chop 'em!" the coach nearest Joey yelled. "Get those knees up! *Hustle!*"

"Whose Mercedes?" Joey asked Frankie, a senior halfback in Joey's squad. Frankie was a returning letterman, one of the camp elite who ate and slept in a separate bunkhouse. Joey had spoken to him before and received only grunts in reply.

"Shut your face," Frankie hissed. "Hustle!" he yelled, echoing the coach, as if trying to hide the fact that he'd spoken to Joey. His cleats splattered mud as he ran briefly in place and then dived sideways.

"Chop 'em up!" bellowed the coach. "Get

those knees high!"

They were doing "monkey rolls." It was Joey's turn to dive. Clear Frankie's pads and roll, under the third guy's dive. Up running. Dive. Roll. Up. Dive. . . .

"Hustle!"

The whistle sounded faster. Dive. Roll. Up running. Dive—

Then Joey's belly seemed to explode. Frankie's cleats slammed into him, digging into his abdomen. The wind went out of Joey in a whoosh.

Choking, he landed on his face and spat out mud. He gagged, trying to get his breath.

"Hustle!" the coach yelled.

Grimly, Joey pushed himself up, slipping in the mud. Getting to his feet, he turned, and saw the Mercedes driving away. Joey saw Frankie glance briefly at the car and then at Joey.

"What were you doing, showing off for the rich guy?" he shouted to Frankie. "Practicing Indian blocks?"

"You want to watch yourself," Frankie replied. "That's how you get hurt, when you don't watch yourself."

The coach's whistle shrilled.

The football camp was on the bank of the Norwich River, a wide, deep stream that flowed down through the mountain forests from across the Canadian border. The water was icy cold, muddy and turbulent from three days of rain. After each early-morning workout the team jogged from the practice field to the riverbank, stripped, and hit the water. Swim across to the float platform, swim back; that was the drill. Rain or shine. The last guy into the water had to do ten extra laps around the practice field at the end of the day. The last guy back on the riverbank had to do twenty.

That morning, just as he'd done the previous days, Joey made sure he wasn't the last in. But once he was over his head in the icy water he found himself struggling. The rain had stopped, but the current was still swift, and Joey's belly cramped where he had been hit. Two guys passed him going out to the raft. As they went by he heard someone scream "Move it!" Looking up, Joey saw Derrick, one of the big offensive tackles and a co-captain, standing on the raft, bellowing at someone nearby. "Move it! You gonna let that turkey beat you?"

Two kids splashed in the water behind him, moving up. Joey swam faster. He was holding his lead as he touched the wet straw on the edge of the raft.

"Move it!" Derrick screamed from above Joey at the two swimmers behind him. "Move it! He's gonna beat you!"

You got it, buddy, Joey thought, determined. He *would* beat them. He made the turn, pushing off hard. His feet slipped a little on the slick steel oil-drum float, setting the raft to rocking.

Something big and heavy thudded onto his back. The impact propelled him down under the brown surface of the river. Gasping by reflex, he inhaled muddy water and choked, his arms flailing frantically. After what seemed an eternity, he came to the surface facing the raft, sputtering and coughing.

Treading water, he saw that Derrick was no longer on the raft. Neither was anyone else. And no one was swimming nearby.

They were still five yards ahead when Joey reached the shallows and waded ashore.

At the edge of the water, the young assistant coach made a mark in his book. "Prescott. Twenty laps tonight."

"Little somethin' to look forward to, Prescott!" someone taunted. He thought he recognized Frankie's voice.

His face burning, Joey only nodded to the assistant coach, but he felt a rush of anger. What was wrong with the coach? How could he let some big jerk jump off the float like that and then make Joey pay the price?

Cool it, he thought. The coach probably hadn't seen anything. The raft was forty yards out in the water and there were nearly a hundred swimmers to keep track of. The coach most likely didn't know what was going on.

But, Joey thought grimly to himself,

there's no way I'm just going to sit by and take this. The way he handled himself now would make all the difference in the way the team thought of him for the rest of the season.

You didn't live in five towns in seven years without learning that most people judged you by their first impression.

Quickly Joey closed the distance between himself and Derrick, heading up the rocky riverbank to where the others were standing in the tall grass, toweling off.

"Hey, Derrick," Joey said, coming around in front of the big lineman. "What happened out there?"

Derrick straightened up. He was about six feet four, bulkier and nearly half a head taller than Joey, with stringy blond hair and squinty eyes and shoulders pitted with acne scars. "Whaddaya mean, what happened?"

Joey took a step closer, up the hill. His head was roughly level with Derrick's chest. He flashed a disarming grin. "Did you see where you landed when you jumped off that raft?"

"No. Where'd I land?" the bully asked.

"You landed on my back, Derrick." The others were edging closer to listen in. Joey kept his voice even. "Your big feet landed right on my back."

Derrick looked down at him. The difference in their heights was exaggerated because Derrick had backed away and was standing farther up the grassy embankment. "You're the new kid, aren't you?" A sneer spread slowly across his fat face.

"You couldn't tell before? Before, when your big feet landed smack on my back, you didn't know I was the new kid?"

"Maybe," Derrick said. "What of it?"

"How much do you weigh, Derrick?"

"Two forty. What of it?"

"Do you know what it's like having two hundred forty pounds land on your back?"

"Hey, kid, I'm a lineman! You think I don't know about guys landin' on my back?"

Joey spotted his opportunity. He grinned and shifted his stance, as if he was about to turn and walk away. "I guess it happens to you linemen all the time, right?"

"Two forty's nothin'. Sometimes we — "

Derrick stopped in surprise as Joey grabbed the big lineman's wrist, pivoted, ducked, and heaved downward, yanking Derrick off balance. Being on lower ground made the move easier than Joey had expected. His hip acted as a fulcrum and Derrick tumbled over him, landing on his back with a thud.

"That was two hundred forty pounds landing on its back," Joey said. "I guess you didn't mind."

Behind him, the others were laughing. Derrick's face flushed crimson as he got to his feet. "Yo, Derrick!" someone shouted.

"You're not gonna take that, right?"

His blue eyes cold, his face twisted with anger, Derrick started for Joey.

"Hold it!" someone yelled. "There's Wynn's car!"

The crowd fell abruptly silent. The big lineman stopped and turned, guilt replacing anger on his face. The gray Mercedes had come into view and stopped at the edge of the grass, hovering near the gathering of swimsuit-clad boys like a shark watching prey. For a moment they didn't move. Then Derrick pushed past Joey on his way to pick up his towel and uniform. "You got lucky, Prescott," he said through clenched teeth. "See how long it lasts."

Joey ignored him and stared at the car. *Who is in there? And why are these guys so afraid of him?*

"Wynn's car," they'd said.

Walking back toward camp a few moments later, Joey asked Andy, "Who's this Wynn, anyway?"

"*Mr.* Wynn," said Andy, nodding at the Mercedes. "He's a great guy."

"Does he own the sporting goods store?"

Andy gave him a look of pure astonishment. "Of course he does. He built it and runs it. Everybody in town knows and is grateful. You'd better hope he likes you. They say he has an eye for who's going to make the team. He can make or break you."

Chapter Two

Back at the bunkhouse, Joey quickly hung up his pads and jersey and put on clean gym shorts and a T-shirt. He was lacing up his sneakers when Andy Blair sat down beside him on the bunk. Andy was a little heavier than Joey and didn't have Joey's quickness or coordination. Red-haired, his smooth pink skin freckled by the sun, Andy was one of those naturally cheerful people you like to be with, even though sometimes you have to help them a little:

"I couldn't believe it," Andy said, his voice hushed but gleeful. "I saw it, but I couldn't believe it."

"What?"

"You know what I mean. Derrick. You really stuck it to him."

"Forget it. It was no big deal."

"Well, you better watch out for him," Andy said. "You don't want to let him keep you from a starting spot. Not from somethin' *that* important! Not when you've got such a good chance. Man, what I'd give if I had a chance as good as yours to make the starting team! But," he added wistfully, "I'd need to be as good as you, wouldn't I?"

Joey turned to look at his friend. "Just keep plugging. You'll make it. That's what I'm gonna do. Let's go get some chow."

Walking together out of the bunkhouse, each was absorbed in his own thoughts of what the morning would bring. After breakfast would be chalk talk. Then a half-hour break for cleanup of the bunkhouse. At ten thirty they would put on the pads again and start another workout, drills at individual positions. Then group drills. Then team drills, offense against defense.

In the mess hall Joey and Andy separated. Joey went to the tables reserved for the offensive team and Andy to the tables where the defensive players ate. The idea, the coach had said when camp had first begun, was to get you functioning as a unit with the guys who would be playing beside you.

The head coach said grace before the waiters brought the food. The waiters at the Norwich High camp weren't what Joey had expected: they were the returning varsity lettermen.

Today the letterman waiting on Joey's table was Frankie. He set down the tray and unloaded bowls of hot cereal and plates of scrambled eggs and ham. "This one's for you, Prescott," he said quietly, handing

Joey his plate. "Special delivery from Derrick."

On top of the eggs was a pile of white powder that looked like salt. At the center of the bowl of cereal was a puddle of something red. The bowl had a peppery scent, like chili powder. The red puddle was probably Tabasco sauce, Joey thought.

"Derrick likes a joke, does he?" Joey said, keeping his voice down so he wouldn't be heard at the coaches' table. "If he wants to joke around he ought to come over and do it himself, don't you think?"

He set the plate and bowl carefully back on Frankie's tray.

Joey felt good for a moment. He had kept his temper and Frankie had shown himself to be a potential friend by warning Joey that the food had come from Derrick. And now he thought he noticed a glint of respect in Frankie's eyes. Was that the same look he'd seen earlier on the field during agility drills? He thought it was.

But all Frankie replied was, "I'll tell him what you said, Prescott."

"And maybe you'll bring some more breakfast for our friend?" Chris asked from beside Joey. "Or do we have to split up our portions so he can have some food?"

"Maybe," said Frankie, a little nervous now. Chris's voice was the kind that carried, and the coaches were looking their way. He gathered up his tray hurriedly.

But as Frankie passed the coaches' table, Coach Gill, the young assistant coach who had been on morning swim duty, stopped him. "Where are you going with that food?"

"Extra portion, sir."

"Extra? Wait a moment, Frankie." Coach Gill stood up and glanced at Joey's table, at the empty placemat where Joey was sitting. Then he looked down at the eggs and the cereal on Frankie's tray. Carefully he took his spoon and tasted a tiny bit of the cereal.

Others were watching now. A hush fell over the mess hall as they waited for the coach's reaction.

Coach Gill made a face. Quickly he reached for his water glass and drank. "All right, Frankie. Are you responsible for this?"

"Yes, sir."

"I find that hard to believe. If you—"

"It was Derrick!" yelled Chris. "He said so himself!"

Derrick was brought over to the coaches' table. The big lineman's arms bulged under his T-shirt as he stood at attention facing Coach Gill. There was almost absolute silence.

"Is it true that you prepared this bowl of cereal, Derrick?"

"Yes, sir."

The coach took another swallow of water and wiped his mouth with his hand. "I'm pleased to see that you're truthful, Derrick.

Tonight after practice you can do twenty extra laps around the field."

He paused, looked across at Joey's table, and added, "You can do them with Prescott."

Joey could see a glitter of malicious satisfaction in Derrick's close-set eyes. *Eyes like a pig,* Joey thought. Suddenly he wondered, *Why did Derrick go after me in the water? Why did he single me out?*

"C'mon, Prescott." In front of Joey, Chris held a plate piled high with runny scrambled eggs and butter-soaked toast. Joey's stomach churned. "C'mon, Prescott. Gotta eat."

"Thanks," he mumbled, taking the plate.

That afternoon the offensive unit went against the defense in a scrimmage game. Joey played far better than any of the other backs, breaking away for four touchdown runs and throwing a halfback option pass nearly forty yards for another score. Today he was in the groove. Other guys on the team noticed, and during the practice he got some compliments, even from Frankie Olivetti, the returning varsity halfback.

Nonetheless, when practice ended at sunset he still had twenty laps to run. Five miles. Joey and Derrick met with Coach Gill in the shadow of the tall pines at the far end of the practice field. "You should finish before dark," the coach said, looking at the clouds overhead. "The faster you run, the faster you get done. Take off your pads ... and see if you can stay ahead of the mosquitoes." With a glance at his watch, and at both of them, he added, "I'll be back to check on you in about forty minutes."

He left them alone on the field. In the waning light, Joey undressed, keeping an eye on Derrick. First, off with the helmet. Then the practice pants and hip pads.

"Gimme a hand, will ya?" Derrick asked, raising his arms and bending forward for Joey to help him off with his practice jersey. Rivulets of sweat ran through the dirt caked on his face, and the greasy black No-Glare on his cheekbones accented the glitter of his piggy eyes.

A V-formation of geese came honking noisily overhead in the darkening sky. The clamor got on Joey's nerves and he tugged hard at Derrick's shirt. *Is there going to be a fight?* he wondered. *What does this guy want?* The mud-covered practice jersey finally came off in Joey's hands, and Derrick quickly shrugged off his shoulder pads and dropped them on the pile with his other gear. In his filthy T-shirt, shorts, and cleats he held out his hands to Joey. "Okay, Prescott. Your turn. Let's get 'em off."

Suddenly it flashed into Joey's mind what Derrick was about to do. He couldn't explain why, he just saw it coming—Derrick's big hands grabbing his jersey, pulling forward, and the moment the fabric was over Joey's head and he couldn't see, the big hands would slam Joey's shoulders down and Derrick's knee would come up to catch him in the face.

"Let's get 'em off! C'mon, don't you trust me?" Derrick's breath came faster now. He was excited. He had Joey out here alone in the darkening shadows, there was nobody around to interfere....

"I'll trust you as far as I threw you this morning," Joey said. "Let's get it over with." *And you can take that any way you want,* he thought. He raised his arms as Derrick grabbed his shirttails and stumbled as Derrick's heave pulled him off balance. *Now it will come,* he thought, readying himself to spin sideways.

But it wasn't the move Joey had expected. Instead, Derrick kicked Joey's feet out from under him and then slammed him into the mud and piled on, fists battering Joey's midsection. "How do you like it, sneak?" Derrick snarled as Joey rolled free. "You're gonna learn somethin' tonight—"

Joey struggled to get the jersey off his head. As Derrick charged, he flung the muddy cloth into his face and jumped to one side, tripping the big lineman and sending him sprawling. "Don't be stupid, Derrick," he said, trying to sound reasonable as Derrick got to his feet. "What can we do here if we fight? Hurt each other? What good will that do? We're both seniors, this is our last year."

"You're the one's gonna get hurt, Prescott. This time you're not gonna get away!" roared Derrick, lunging at him.

Moments later they were down in the dirt, locked in a vicious struggle. Now there was only the rasping of hard, painful breath and the honking of the geese overhead, the ebb and surge of strength from within, and finally the awakening of real fear in Joey as he realized he was weakening, that he couldn't hold his own much longer, and that his opponent's power seemed undiminished. Rancid breath and sour-smelling sweat poured from the lineman and his eyes shone with malicious triumph. "Gonna remember tonight, Prescott. Gonna remember."

He's crazy, Joey thought. *Crazy enough to kill me.* He struggled harder, but now Derrick's thick fingers were digging into his windpipe—

Suddenly Derrick went limp. To Joey's amazement his eyes widened with what looked like fear. Pushing Joey away from him, he scrambled to his feet.

Gasping for breath, Joey rolled over on his hands and knees and looked up.

The Mercedes was parked about fifteen yards away.

Joey wondered. Had he been watching them the whole time?

The door of the car opened. A man was getting out. Joey shivered as he tried to catch his breath. Still on hands and knees, he watched, fascinated. This man was somehow different from anyone he had ever seen.

It wasn't his clothes that made him different, though they were certainly elegant and expensive. He was dressed all in brown. A long brown leather coat, a brown hat, brown driving gloves, a brown suit, gleaming brown shoes ... everything was the same rich color, like coffee with cream. His white shirt and white tie looked crisp and stiff, like armor.

Was it the man's face? Yellow skin stretched over high cheekbones, a thick black mustache that nearly hid his mouth, snapping black eyes ... or was it the way he moved? Getting out of the car, he appeared to grow larger, and as he came toward the two boys he seemed to glide.

Joey had the feeling that a powerful drug had taken control of his senses. His limbs seemed to float free of his body and his impressions were distorted and confused. For some reason he remembered something that had happened years ago when they'd lived in Florida. Fishing in a friend's rowboat, Joey'd jumped in to do some snorkeling and had seen a barracuda. It had hovered, silent and motionless, in the water, watching Joey with its hard, flat eye, and Joey had known right then who was master in those waters and who had better get out while there was still time.

With a gigantic effort, Joey dragged himself to his feet, forcing his thoughts away from this long-ago encounter, and extended a hand to the approaching Mr. Wynn.

"Prescott, isn't it?" asked the man in a deep, resonant voice. "I hear you did pretty well in today's scrimmage."

"It was a good day, sir," answered Joey. He was surprised to hear his voice so calm. *Now what came over me?* he asked himself. *What just happened?*

"Call me Mr. Wynn. If you make the starting team you'll call me by a different name. Isn't that right, Derrick?"

Derrick's big head bobbed. "Yes, sir."

"Tell me, Joey . . . do you think you'll have more good days like you had today?"

"I hope to, sir—Mr. Wynn, I mean."

"Good." He nodded, pleased, and below the thick mustache his teeth momentarily showed white against his skin. In the fading light it looked like yellowed parchment. Joey wondered how old the man was. "You've got talent, Prescott. We want to make full use of our talent. That's where victories come from, from making full use of our talent. Isn't that right, Derrick?"

Derrick's head bobbed again, as if by reflex. "Yes, sir."

Mr. Wynn continued in the same pleasant, richly modulated tone. "And when one of us does something that's not for the good of the team, that presents a problem, doesn't it, Derrick? A problem that must be dealt with?"

"Sir, I thought—"

"Yes, Derrick? What did you think?"

Derrick hesitated, then moved closer to Mr. Wynn and said something that Joey could not hear. "I guess I was wrong," he added.

"Sometimes people rush into things," Mr. Wynn said. "They get a little carried away and don't realize what they're really doing until it's too late. You wouldn't want to be one of those people, would you, Derrick?"

"No, sir."

"Good. Now I believe you have five miles to run." His nod dismissed Derrick, but he motioned Joey to stay. "Now, Joey Prescott, I hope you also will profit from today's exchange." He watched Derrick round the first turn behind the goalposts at a near-sprint. Then he studied Joey more closely. "Do you know, I can't help thinking that we may have seen each other before. Do you suppose it's just the fading light out here?"

The barracuda suspended in the blue haze.

Joey forced the image out of his mind. "I don't know, Mr. Wynn. I've lived in a number of different towns. We've only moved into Norwich this summer."

"Indeed?" Again Joey saw that brief, pleased expression, the look of a master happy with a clever pupil. *Why?*

"—I've seen a good bit of the world myself," Mr. Wynn was saying. "I think we're going to get along, Prescott. I also think you will be more pleased with Norwich than you expect. Provided you continue your present course, I think you can look forward to a good deal of success."

There was a moment's awkward silence when Joey couldn't think of anything to say.

"Thank you, Mr. Wynn," he said finally.

Mr. Wynn nodded toward the track, where Derrick was coming out of the backstretch, still at a fast pace. "I also think you're going to run those five miles at a clip that will surprise you. Now get moving and keep up the good work."

When Coach Gill emerged from the forest trail and called out "Forty minutes," it was almost too dark to see him. Both Joey and Derrick were on their final lap around the field. The two had not spoken a word, not even when Joey had caught up with Derrick and passed him.

The coach watched them finish. "You two don't look tired," he said. "You sure you've done the whole twenty?"

Chapter Three

They washed in the big utility sink outside the mess hall. "Still got time for supper," called Coach Gill. Standing beside Derrick, Joey cupped his hands under the cold spring water and drank deeply, then lathered his hands with the big brown bar of laundry soap and scrubbed his face. The coach threw clean towels to both of them. "Okay, now. Walk in there side by side ... and no more nonsense."

A hush fell over the diners. Joey's heart pounded as he felt their eyes on him. He was still on his feet, his face was unmarked: how had he done it? That would be the question all of them were asking themselves. Chris elbowed him when he sat down. "Hey, Prescott. We thought you were gonna come in doing one of these—" He stuffed his mouth full of blueberry pie and grinned blearily. "You kick his butt or what?"

"Nobody kicked anybody," Joey said wearily.

"You throw him again? He show any guts this time?"

"Nobody threw anybody. Let's just say it's settled, okay? We both have better things to do than fight."

Across the table, Larry Dewinter leaned forward. "Save the crap for the enemy, right? Put *them* on their behinds." Others at the table nodded in agreement. Chris passed a platter with two lamb chops and mashed potatoes. "We saved *this* crap for *you*, Prescott."

Trudging through the wet grass on the way back to the bunkhouse that night, Andy Blair spoke to Joey in awed tones. He'd never seen a new kid do as well as Joey had done that day. A star performance in the scrimmage and putting that Derrick in his place . . .

"Forget it," said Joey.

"Nobody else is gonna forget it," insisted Andy. "You'll see. Wait till closing night! When the cheerleaders and the student government and the band come up around the big campfire they're all gonna hear about the new kid, Joey Prescott. Your name's gonna be on that starting roll, I just know it!

"I just wish I could say the same about yours truly, but no matter how hard I try—" He broke off, shaking his head. "But I'm gonna keep plugging just like we said this morning."

"That's all anybody can do," Joey agreed. He was depressed by Andy's certainty of being doomed by his poor performance in today's scrimmage. The day had divided the friends — made one a winner and one a loser. Somebody's got to win and somebody's got to lose, the coaches all said. The job here at camp was making sure the loser was the other guy — and then, once the season started, the other *team*.

Joey got better and better with every practice. He and Frankie blocked for each other with good, accurate timing. "It's like you got radar," Coach Gill said enthusiastically one afternoon. Time passed in a blur of drills and plays, sprints and hits and catches, moments of pain and moments of satisfaction. No one bothered Joey; even Derrick kept his distance.

Still, on the last day of camp, when the time came for the final scrimmage, Joey had a bellyful of butterflies. What if he fumbled? What if he threw an interception? What if someone nailed him and he broke his ankle? When he gained eighteen yards his first carry, the butterflies disappeared. He was no longer self-conscious. As the game progressed he had moments when he felt that he was seeing the action on the field from high above, that he was just sitting back and watching the field as if it were a chessboard and the players were pawns. He saw himself, even as he ran, and knew he would score just as surely as if he were watching a TV replay.

Despite the exhilarating feeling, Joey worried that he might be heading for a fall because he wasn't concentrating. Yet he *was* concentrating, that was the weird thing. He was just seeing more of what was there to see. . . .

And not once did he fumble.

During a time-out he noticed Mr. Wynn. He was wearing his leather coat and standing with Mr. Leach, the burly old head coach who had been at Norwich for nearly a dozen years. For a moment Joey thought that Mr. Leach was asking a question and that Mr. Wynn had nodded out toward the field and said, "Prescott," but that was impossible, Joey told himself, because he hadn't actually *heard* anything. You couldn't hear from this distance anyway unless it was a real yell.

The quarterback called Joey's number two plays later and Joey ran thirty-six yards for a touchdown, beating Moltzie in a footrace for the goal line. Power seemed to flow into his legs, hurling him forward. He'd never felt so strong in his life. Coming back to the huddle, he saw Mr. Wynn nod slightly as if to congratulate him.

That night's dinner was their last in camp

and a festive affair. The school marching band arrived in gaudy red uniforms and set up at the head of the hall. After the meal the wooden rafters shook with school fight songs. Then three shapely and acrobatic girls in cheerleaders' outfits appeared and the hall erupted in cheers. One of the girls, a tall redhead, smiled as if she'd seen it all before as she stepped up to the microphone. The others would be along soon, she said, but, meanwhile, how about yelling like you mean it? The uproar was deafening.

Before the closing ceremony was scheduled to begin they had an hour's free time. Walking along the forest road with Andy, Joey tried to buoy his friend's spirits. The night was clear and crisp, with a light frost covering the ground. "Hayride weather," said Andy glumly. "Just look at that moon. . . . You're gonna have your pick, you know that? And me, I'm gonna be nowhere. My senior year and I'll probably have to rob the cradle."

"Aw, c'mon. Plenty of girls don't give two hoots about football."

"You obviously don't know the girls here," grumbled Andy, dislodging a rock with the toe of his shoe and sending it skittering away into the darkness. "That's *all* they're interested in."

"Baloney."

"I'm telling you the truth. They're all alike. Maybe one or two exceptions, tops. If you're a starter, the word is they'll do *any-thing* for you. If you're not . . . well, I've got plenty of experience with *that* category—"

"Look," said Joey sternly, "how many girls are in the school? And how many starters? Unless there are only twenty-two girls there's got to be some left over."

Retracing their steps along the dark road, they heard a car behind them. Stepping aside to let it pass, Andy suddenly cried, "Harriet!" A red MG two-seater draped in red and white crepe paper stopped a few yards beyond them and backed up. The top was down and behind the wheel sat one of the two best-looking girls Joey had ever seen. The other was in the passenger's seat. Dressed in cheerleaders' sweaters, they looked like athletes; gymnasts, Joey thought.

"Hi, Andy," said the girl who was driving, a blonde. "We haven't seen you since camp started. How've you been?"

"Great," replied Andy, grabbing Joey by the arm and pushing him forward. "I'd like you to meet my friend Joey Prescott. Joey, this is Harriet," he said, indicating the blonde "—and this is Bonnie." Joey was momentarily tongue-tied. He couldn't take his eyes off the dark-haired, dark-eyed girl.

"Well," said Harriet, shifting the car into first, "we've got to get up to the camp and help set up. I'd offer you two a ride but as you can see, we don't have much room.

Spike here" — she waved her arm to indicate a small white bulldog crouching behind the seats — "takes up all the space."

As the girls roared off, Andy explained that Spike was the team mascot.

"Enough about the dog," groaned Joey. "Just tell me about the girls!"

Andy cast a sidelong glance at his friend and smiled. "The girls, huh? In fact, those two are practically the only ones in town who aren't football crazy. That's why they stick together. They're intellectuals or something . . . y'know, they don't think they have to go out with the football players or anything."

Joey was puzzled. "What do you mean, 'have to'?"

"Oh, it's a tradition. If a guy's on the starting team he doesn't get turned down for a date. It's not like a girl would go to jail or anything, it's just that —"

"You mean to tell me that those two have never been asked out by anyone on the team?" Joey was confused.

"Well," explained Andy, "they've sort of been 'taken' — Bonnie's been dating Steve Ward, the student government president, and Harriet's been going out with Bill Elverson, the captain of the basketball team. But no one knows what would happen if they were asked. . . ."

"What *could* happen if they said no?" pressed Joey. "Would they be kicked off the cheerleading squad? Flunk gym?"

"That's just it," said Andy. "Nobody knows. It hasn't happened before ... at least, not since Norwich became the state champion."

The flickering flames of the ceremonial campfire were in sight. "Anyway," continued Andy, "don't get your hopes up. Those two weren't around when Norwich's winning streak began. They moved to town a few seasons later, but they never really got bitten by the football bug. Too different. Too involved in their studies or something. If there's a beer party after the ceremony, you can bet those two won't be sticking around. Neither of them drinks beer. But," he added with a sigh, "I bet you'll find some others who'll make you forget 'em."

"*We'll* find some others," corrected Joey.

Andy shook his head as they approached the circle around the fire. "Don't I wish. But let's not kid ourselves." He jammed his hands into his pockets. "The only way I'm gonna be a starter is if Moltzie or Hefferman breaks a leg."

Joey and Andy sat together during the speeches by the assistant coaches. Tension increased by the minute. The only sound besides the speaker's voice was the slow chirp of the crickets. Around the fire, faces were rapt. The band members and the cheerleaders listened just as intently as the football players as the coaches talked about the competitive world, about keeping the town on the map, about getting respect for the name of Norwich and molding a future the community could be proud of. *They really believe this stuff*, Joey thought. Maybe his mother was right when she said that everyone in Norwich was a fanatic about football. He saw Bonnie sitting with the other cheerleaders. Was she as taken in as the others? he wondered. It was hard to tell.

When the coach began to unfold the piece of paper, Joey's mouth was dry. His pulse was hammering in his temples and he felt a tightness in his throat. He turned to Andy to say "Well, here we go," but he never said it. Andy's eyes were shut as if he was praying, and his whole body trembled. At that moment Joey would have traded places with Andy if he could.

The names of the offense were read first. One by one the players stood and acknowledged the cheers as their names were called. When the coach said "Prescott," Joey felt a surge of warmth throughout his body. Andy's fingers dug into his arm as he pushed Joey to his feet. As he stood looking around at the cheering, firelit faces, Joey heard Andy saying, "Way to go, way to go, way to go," in a voice choked with emotion.

Next came the names of the defensive unit. Joey held his breath. The coach would say "Blair" or he wouldn't and that would be it.

"Alexander ... Bartlett ... Cramer ..."

Joey felt numb. So Andy had been right. He didn't want to look down to where his friend was sitting.

When it was time for the twenty-two starting players to move to the front of the campfire, though, Joey couldn't help seeing him. His eyes bulged and his lips were pressed hard together. He was staring blankly ahead, unmindful of the tears that poured down his cheeks.

After the ceremony, those who hadn't made the lineup stayed behind at the campfire for a special talk from Coach Leach. Joey went with the other starters and Coach Gill to the starters' bunkhouse. There, stacked neatly on two of the cots, were twenty-two large white boxes. "Mr. Wynn left these for you," explained the coach. Joey saw his name stenciled on one of the boxes in big black letters. "They're your varsity jackets. Wear them with pride."

The players moved forward to claim their boxes. No one spoke. Scotch tape snapped and cardboard rattled as the cartons came open. Joey saw a flash of red beneath the white tissue paper and smelled the unmistakable scent of leather. For a moment he just savored the fragrance, and then his fingers were digging beneath the filmy paper and pulling out the jacket. It *was* real leather, thick red suede for the body and

33

supple white kidskin for the sleeves. He ran his fingertips over the smooth satin lining. Slipping it on, he fastened the front snaps and wondered at the perfect fit. He had never worn such an expensive jacket. The only thing he didn't like was the white patch on the chest bearing the face of a bulldog. Its eyes reminded him of Derrick's. But, he told himself, what could you do when the team was called the Bulldogs?

"For all you new boys," the coach said, "Mr. Wynn went by the height and weight marked on your medical chart to get your size. If the jacket doesn't fit just right he wants you to bring it with you when you come to practice Monday morning."

Wasn't Monday Labor Day? Joey was about to ask, but then the coach went on, "That's Labor Day, as you know. You boys who are returning from last year will remember what happens after practice. You boys who are new — well, you'll find out soon enough. For now I'll just tell you not to plan anything for that day until the afternoon."

"What happens Labor Day?" Joey asked Frankie.

"A team secret," Frankie told him with a wink. Joey had the feeling that it couldn't be bad.

Leaving the bunkhouse, Joey walked with two starters who were trying to decide whether they should wear their jackets to the party by the river or drop them off at the bunkhouse. Joey was about to ask them about the party when he saw Andy walking away from the campfire, his shoulders hunched and his head down. "See you guys in a minute," said Joey, taking off after his friend.

Andy heard his footsteps on the dirt path and looked up, but he didn't stop walking. When Joey was alongside, Andy cleared his throat. "How was it?"

"Okay. No big deal." Joey caught his breath, feeling awkward. Suddenly it seemed as if Andy had been right; that they *would* be apart now and that nothing could be done about it.

"How was your meeting?" he asked, trying to sound casual.

"Same as last year." There was a pause. "The jacket looks great on you," said Andy wistfully. "You're gonna be a star." He cleared his throat again. "Don't worry about me, I'm okay. I'm not gonna quit. Maybe I'll get a service letter out of it. They give some guys a letter if they stick it out for all four years."

The MG approached Joey's group as they walked toward the river. Bonnie and Harriet waved politely but they were obviously going back to town. Joey waved back, disappointed.

"Yo! Turn around!" Frankie yelled, blocking their path, holding his last year's varsity jacket in front of him like a bullfighter's cape. But Harriet drove past without slowing down and Frankie had to dodge to get out of the way. "Crazy broad," Frankie muttered. "But you'll see," he said, looking at Joey. "She'll come to me. I like 'em with a little spirit, you know?"

"Who? Harriet?"

"Yeah. The blonde. Why? You want the dark-haired one?"

"No," Joey lied.

"Hey," said Frankie, changing the subject, "watch out for Derrick tonight. I wouldn't want to be putting on the blindfold with you guys. Not with him around."

"What blindfold?" Joey was suddenly nervous.

"You'll find out," said Frankie with a grin, clapping him on the back. They were at the edge of the practice field now.

"Another 'team secret'?"

"Don't worry about it." Frankie went on talking casually as he eyed two pretty majorettes heading toward them. "The trick is to be feeling no pain, if you know what I mean."

Joey was watching a scene on the edge of the riverbank. Derrick was sitting on the roof of a station wagon with one of the cheerleaders and both of them were looking down at another cheerleader.

ensued, Derrick against the cheerleaders. One at a time the girls would climb up onto the roof of the car, sit beside Derrick, pop open two beers, and hand one to him. At the count of three the two contestants would go to it, swilling down the beer as fast as they could. Each contest ended the same way: the girl would be sputtering and choking and Derrick would have his can turned upside down to show it was empty.

Joey counted ten cheerleaders. Derrick had drunk ten cans of beer in less than fifteen minutes. Where was he putting it?

"Yo!" Derrick was looking around for his next opponent, but it seemed as though the cheerleaders had all had enough. "*I* know!" The big lineman stood up unsteadily on the hood. "Prescott! Get up here!"

"Forget it!" Joey called back.

Swaying, Derrick put a hand on the roof to steady himself. "Forget *you*, Prescott! What's the matter, no guts?"

Joey had had enough. Stepping forward, he shook his head and said quietly, "You've got a bigger belly than I do, Derrick. And a bigger mouth. I'll admit it. I just don't want to be around when you blow lunch."

From behind him, Tracy added, "And you're hogging all the beer, you big lug!"

Derrick blinked, trying to focus on the owner of the new voice.

Then, without warning, he launched himself forward off the hood of the station wagon, skimming over Joey's head in a flat-out dive for Tracy.

The girls screamed. "Look out!" Joey yelled. Grabbing Derrick in mid-air, he pushed him to one side so that Tracy would not be hit. There was a heavy thud as Derrick landed on the damp grass. Crying, Tracy ran to Joey and buried her face in his chest. "I was so scared, so scared!" she kept saying. Joey put his arm around her.

They all watched silently as Derrick, on hands and knees, spewed up beer in a great rush, like some gargoyle on a fountain. Most of the girls turned away. "Some party, guys," Frankie remarked from behind them.

Derrick got to his feet. Pulling his shirttails out of his belt, he wiped his face and hands. "See?" He held out his hands. "Good as new! You wait till you put on the old blindfold tonight, Prescott! You wait till it's gauntlet time—"

"Shut up, Derrick!" The voice of Larry, middle linebacker and team captain, came like a whipcrack. "That's enough!"

"Yeah? You tell me—"

"That's enough, I said!" Larry and five others were suddenly at Derrick's side, moving him backward, away from the station wagon and the steaming puddle he'd left behind.

"All right, all right, lemme alone!" Derrick yelled. Shaking himself free, he turned away and headed over the edge of the embankment toward the river.

It was cold standing in the moonlight. "What a screwed-up guy," said Tracy as they watched his retreating form.

"Well," sighed Jill, opening the door to her car, "I guess the party's over."

"I guess so," said Tracy, casting a glance at the pile of empty beer cans. "Good night, Joey. I hope I'll see you again."

Joey gave her a hug and said he hoped so too.

Soon only the team members were left on the field.

Larry looked around at the faces of the starters, twenty now that Derrick had disappeared. "Let's get this done now." He pulled a handful of black cloth strips from his pocket.

"Nine new guys, nine blindfolds. Come up and take yours and put it on. The rest of you form two lines."

Soon Joey and eight others were blindfolded, hands on each other's shoulders. *Like a row of circus elephants*, thought Joey. He heard Larry's voice. "This is to teach you to trust the guys on the team. You understand? You go through the gauntlet, you show you trust us. Also you show us you can take it. You ready?"

A few scattered voices replied, "Ready."

"All right. When it's your turn, you go through with your hands at your sides. Understand? At your sides. Whatever happens, don't raise your hands. You're going to show us what you're made of."

There was a moment's silence. Then the line started to move forward. Joey was last. His skin prickled as he waited for his turn. Ahead he heard grunts, slapping noises, the thud of flesh meeting flesh. He could hear his own breath coming faster, feel the blindfold scratching his cheeks, feel the sweat moistening his palms. From somewhere he heard a cry of pain and then a sudden squeal.

"Okay, Prescott, you're up. Go!"

Blindly, he went forward. Hands grabbed his shoulders and pushed him on. He heard slaps and grunts just ahead, always just ahead—

And then laughter. His blindfold was tugged away and he could see the others laughing. It had all been a joke, nobody'd been hurt; they really *had* been showing them they could be trusted. Joey felt a wave of relief and happiness wash over him and he broke into a wide grin. Now he was certain it was all right, that all the work and sweat and worry of camp was worth it when it paid off in a moment like this.

Joey wished that Andy were there to join in the laughter. Of all the guys at camp there was probably no one who would have savored the moment more than Andy. . . .

"Hey," broke in one of the guys, "somebody's coming back." Quieting down, the group watched as a pair of headlight beams spread a yellow swath across the moon-silvered grass.

It was Jill's red station wagon. Looking a bit scared and not at all intoxicated, Jill rolled down her window. "Have you seen Spike?" she asked. "We've lost him and it's all my fault!"

In the confusion following the party the cheerleaders had driven away without the school's bulldog mascot. No one had seen him. "You girls stay in the car," said Larry. "We'll fan out and search the area."

Joey headed for the riverbank. He didn't have any set plan in mind, he just went down half expecting to see the dog drinking at the water's edge. The moon made a shimmering pathway across the river and whitened the rocks that littered the shallows. Even with this light, Joey thought, there were hundreds of spots where a dog could hide. How could they ever find him?

Then he saw a dark stain on top of a large rock. Without thinking he went closer and touched it. It was warm and sticky and there were bits of something white embedded in it.

Bending down to rinse off his hands in the water, Joey saw the cream-colored body of the dog. It had been shoved underneath the rock, half in the water, half out, and its back legs were bobbing gently in the slow current. When Joey saw the head he realized with a shudder that the dark stain was blood and the white particles were pieces of skull mingled with the dog's brains.

Derrick was lying on his back nearby, apparently asleep, clutching a bloody rock.

His eyes riveted on the rock, Joey put two fingers in his mouth and whistled for the others to come.

The noise roused Derrick a little. He moved slightly and spoke in a drugged voice. "That's you someday, Prescott. You can count on it."

Chapter Four

Monday morning Joey woke up to the smell of fresh air. For a moment he imagined he was still at football camp, but when he opened his eyes he saw his posters, his trophies, the yellowing walls of this room. He remembered. Today was Labor Day.

And there was football practice at eight A.M. His digital clock read 7:00 and school was a half hour's bicycle ride. As he dressed he began to remember the events of the previous evening. Derrick had been loaded into the back seat of Coach Leach's Cadillac, his head lolling forward and his chin covered with spittle. When they had lifted him from the riverbank the rock had fallen from Derrick's hand and rolled into the water.

Downstairs, Joey's mother had the kitchen window open. As she spooned neat circles of pancake batter onto the hot cast-iron griddle she looked fondly at her son. "Nice to have clean air for a change, isn't it?" she asked. Slender and brisk, she wore jeans and a freshly pressed blouse and had her hair pinned up. A breeze ruffled the curtains that she washed every week to keep white. "Your father's off to an early start this morning so we'll eat alone."

In his most recent job, Joey's dad traveled to restaurants in the three counties surrounding Norwich selling novelty items. Labor Day weekend and other holidays he was kept busy checking the restaurants near the highways, making certain none had run out of stock. Before, Joey's dad had sold shoes, used cars, encyclopedias, and soft drink vending machines, among other things. The job that had looked the most promising was three jobs back, when they'd moved to the suburbs just outside Boston and he had sold office equipment. But the job hadn't lasted more than three months. Joey didn't know why. He didn't know why *any* of the jobs hadn't lasted, but he'd come to recognize the signs when one was about to end. His mother would have a worried look for a few days and there'd be raised voices behind his parents' bedroom door, and then one day he'd come home from school and find his dad at the kitchen table, looking at library photocopies of newspaper classifieds from different towns and pecking out letters on the little portable typewriter.

Coach Leach gathered them together in the

locker room. The first thing Joey noticed was that Derrick wasn't there and that Randy Overmeir, already wearing a varsity jacket, had taken his place.

The second thing he noticed was a young bulldog, with a spike collar and large lower teeth, being led out of the coaches' room by Coach Gill.

"About Saturday night, boys," the coach began. The room was instantly silent. "How many of you have said anything to anyone about what happened? Raise your hands."

No hands went up. That night down by the riverbank Larry had made it very clear. The bulldog's death was to be a "team secret." Not even the girls were to be told; they still thought that Spike had just wandered off.

"Good," continued the coach. "I don't have to tell you to keep it that way. I also think you know as well as I do what happens when a team wins seven state championships in a row, but I'll mention it just the same to refresh your memories. People start gunning for you, boys! They want to knock off Norwich and they'll look high and low for dirt they can use to make us look bad. It means we have to be extra careful, both in what we do and who we talk to. I'm not saying you can't have a good time, boys, because as starting team members I hope and believe you're going to have the best time of your young lives this fall. But what I am saying is that you should be careful. Are there any questions? Does everyone understand what I'm telling you?"

Frankie raised his hand. "Will Derrick be coming to practices?"

The coach shook his head. "Derrick has gone away. He'll be away for quite some time, probably several months. When he returns, I think he'll be a changed young man. I *do* know he will be receiving the best of care and that his emotional difficulties will be given the finest medical attention. And when he does return, I want all of you to remember him as he was before any of these recent incidents began. In fact, it would be best for all of us to simply put those incidents out of our minds. Do you follow me, boys?" He leaned forward, his nostrils flaring. "Those incidents *never happened.*"

Alone at the entrance to the field house, Joey waited for Mr. Wynn's Mercedes to arrive. He was the first of the ten new boys — ten counting Randy Overmeir — to be taken for a visit to Wynn's Sporting Goods store.

He didn't know why he'd been selected to go first and he didn't know what the visit was about. All he knew was that at ten o'clock Mr. Wynn himself would pick him up and that under no circumstances was he to be late. Taking no chances, he was out on the corner of Main Street and School Road five minutes early.

For the hundredth time he wondered about Derrick. What was *wrong* with the kid? Had it been just the beer? Why had he gone off the deep end that way? And why had he said, "That's you, Prescott"?

Why?

Those incidents never happened.

But they *had* happened, and Derrick would be coming back. And when he did come back, what was to prevent him from drinking too much some other night and—

"Prescott?"

The voice startled Joey. Whirling around, he saw the gray Mercedes stopped at the curb. The car had come up School Road, so Joey hadn't noticed its approach. It waited, motor purring. Behind the wheel, Mr. Wynn leaned toward the open window on the passenger's side. "Joey Prescott, are you ready?"

The interior of the Mercedes was gray leather. Cold dry air poured from the chrome air-conditioner vents, giving the car a metallic smell. Although the blower was on high, Joey could hear Mr. Wynn's deep voice clearly as he said, "They tell me you were the one who found the dog."

Joey swallowed. "Yes, sir—" He stopped. "The coach says the incident never happened, sir."

"That's the position we're taking if any outsiders should ask." Mr. Wynn slid his eyes from the road to meet Joey's. "You needn't worry about me, Joey. I'm a friend of the team. By the way, did you forget? For now you call me Mr. Wynn." Sunlight glazed his face as they drove through an intersection and Joey noticed again how thick and yellowed his skin was. Like some kind of parchment or leather, Joey thought. Despite the bright sun, it was so cold in the car that the small hairs on the back of Joey's neck stood upright. Sinking farther down into the seat, Joey buried his chin in his jacket and shuddered.

"Joey?"

"Sorry, Mr. Wynn. Right." It was odd, but Joey had the sensation that Mr. Wynn wanted him to look at him. Almost forcing himself not to, Joey stared straight ahead, watching the traffic, the old buildings, the dirty bricks and peeling wooden porches and cracked sidewalks of the town.

"Saturday night, Joey. What I want to know is: what did the boy say when you found him?"

Joey debated with himself for a moment. Should he tell him? He hadn't told anyone that Derrick had said anything at all.

Reaching over, Mr. Wynn rested a brown-gloved hand on Joey's knee. It was so incredibly light that the smooth brown leather might have been filled with helium. Joey's throat constricted and he could feel his heart begin to pound.

"His exact words, please," urged Mr. Wynn silkily. His eyes riveted on that gloved hand, Joey had no defense and he heard himself telling the whole story. When he had finished the hand moved away as if it had been a mechanical device that had completed its task of gathering information.

"Good, Joey." Mr. Wynn had both hands on the wheel now. "I'm glad you've decided to trust me. It must have disturbed you hearing Derrick say something like that. Did it disturb you?"

"A little." Joey was uncomfortable answering the man's questions.

"I had been wondering, you see, because considering what Derrick had done he might have said something of a different nature. When people are disturbed the way Derrick is they begin to think in terms of attaining unusual powers that—" He broke off. "Is something the matter with your hand?"

Without realizing it, Joey was wiping the fingers of his left hand on his jeans. "The blood," he said, looking down. "I touched the blood with this hand."

Mr. Wynn nodded sympathetically. "Your memory of this will pass with time, Joey, so long as you aren't afraid to speak of it to those you trust. Do you trust me, Joey?" His voice was persuasive, hypnotic.

"Yes, Mr. Wynn."

Mr. Wynn smiled. "I have a theory about

why poor Derrick killed the dog," he continued in a normal tone of voice. "In some primitive cultures it is believed that taking the life of another confers a special power on the killer. An energy of life is absorbed that makes him feel—"

"Powerful," volunteered Joey.

"Quite so, Joey," said Mr. Wynn approvingly as though he'd found an apt pupil. "Derrick killed the dog because it made him feel powerful."

Joey didn't respond and they drove the rest of the way in silence. Reaching the store, Mr. Wynn nosed the Mercedes down the garage ramp and pressed a button on the dashboard. A black metal door at the bottom of the ramp slid open with a pneumatic hiss. Inside was a huge, brightly lit room lined with row upon row of cartons and crates and machinery, rider-mowers, bicycles, motorbikes—

"How do you like our stockroom?" asked Mr. Wynn, switching off the ignition. Before Joey had a chance to respond, Mr. Wynn continued. "We have a lot here, but it's important, Joey, that material things don't assume too much importance in our lives. As Adam Smith once said, the *real* wealth of any nation—or any city or town, for that matter—is not to be found in its material goods; not in gold or gems or paintings"— he gestured toward a row of cardboard cartons marked SONY—"or in the capital inventory of a man's warehouse stock. The real wealth of a nation is its *people:* their ambitions, their intelligence, their hopes and dreams, their very lives. *That* is true wealth, Joey!"

Joey's skin crawled and he felt that he would suffocate if he stayed in the car another second. Dust seemed to fill his eyes and ears and choke his lungs. He wanted to scream and push it away, but he was powerless under the spell cast by that deep, soothing voice.

Calm down, he told himself. *It's just a history lesson.* "Are you saying that our team is some kind of wealth for the town?" Maybe talking would make him relax, Joey thought.

Mr. Wynn nodded in agreement and turned his big head toward Joey. "Exactly," he purred. "That's exactly what I mean." Looking into the man's eyes, it was all Joey could do to keep from screaming. In the dark eyes of Mr. Wynn he saw a vacuum, a nothingness that threatened to draw him in and never release him.

Glancing away quickly, Joey heard Mr. Wynn laugh softly. "You really are a very perceptive boy, Joey," he said. Beneath the heavy mustache, the tips of his teeth were revealed in a reptilian smile. Joey trembled. "I really do feel that I've known you before," continued Mr. Wynn. "Perhaps in another time. Reincarnation is a kind of hobby of mine. The *study* of reincarnation, that is, not the act itself. It's silly to believe that we could live after death, isn't it, Joey?" He gave Joey a knowing smile.

Then, to Joey's immense relief, he opened the door and got out. "Enough talk, Joey. Let's go sign you up. Follow me."

"Sign me up?" The warehouse was the size of an arena and Joey's voice echoed between the concrete walls. Against one wall was a computer terminal and a chrome steel chair bolted to the floor.

"That's right, Joey. We sign you up. It's a simple ceremony and it has benefits I'll explain in just a moment." Seating himself in the chair, Mr. Wynn pressed several of the number keys in rapid succession. No numbers appeared on the screen.

Then, behind the screen, the wall began to move.

It slid open to reveal a large room, its walls covered with metal drawers. *Like a bank vault,* Joey thought. In the center of the room was a table of chrome steel that looked like an altar of some sort.

"Come on in, Joey." As Joey stepped inside, the wall-door slid shut behind him. Mr. Wynn pointed to the ceiling above the table, where Joey could see a large glass lens and a row of lights. "Have you ever had an X-ray picture taken, Joey?"

He explained. The lens was part of a special camera that, when connected to a computer, took pictures and converted them into exact measurements. For example, the blazers and slacks worn when traveling to away games could be custom-fit for each member of the team with the aid of the computer. "We do the same for your uniforms, of course, including the cleats and warm-up suits. Also," Mr. Wynn went on, "if you decide to buy your school clothes at Wynn's we'll custom-fit those, too. As a team member you can buy anything in our store at wholesale cost; so can any member of your family. Do you have any brothers or sisters, Joey?"

"No. But my parents will be pleased, I'm sure. About the wholesale thing, I mean."

"I'm glad. Now if you'll just take off your shoes and lie down on the table ... Face upward and look at the camera lens ... Good..." Joey's thoughts were a blur. *Is this guy up to something or am I imagining the whole thing?* Numbly, Joey obeyed.

There was a click and a hum and the bank of lights above glowed brightly. Joey felt suddenly weak.

"Now lie on your side, please," Mr. Wynn ordered briskly. "A profile shot. Do you know, natives in some primitive societies are afraid to have their pictures taken? They believe that the photographer will capture their soul in his little black box. Isn't that amusing?" The lights glowed again, the machinery clicked and hummed. "Now the opposite profile and then one face downward and we shall be finished."

About a minute later, Joey climbed down from the table.

"Feel a little dizzy? The bright lights seem to affect people that way sometimes. Now, Joey, there's just one little formality remaining. The signing up. Would you just stand aside one moment, please?"

From a drawer beneath the chromed surface of the table Mr. Wynn lifted out a large book bound in black leather and a gold pen. Then he reached into the interior of the drawer and Joey thought he saw him push a button. There was a whir of machinery and then, from a slot in the end of the table, came a plastic-coated page with Joey's photograph at the top. Joey stared. The quality of the picture was remarkable, far sharper and with more vivid color than anything he had ever seen before. The image actually seemed to be three-dimensional.

"Living color," said Mr. Wynn, satisfied. "You'll notice there is a pledge beneath the photograph. It's the same for all team members. Would you read it aloud, please?"

Joey cleared his throat. "I, Joey Prescott, pledge to give my best to the team." He looked up. "That's it?"

"That's it. Are you ready to sign?"

"Sure," Joey said. "I always give my best anyway."

The pen felt heavy in his hand, but it

wrote smoothly, the ink penetrating the plastic coating of the paper. "There are some very important people in here," said Mr. Wynn, sliding the page into the book and closing it. "Some names you would recognize immediately. You have a good future ahead of you, Joey. Welcome aboard."

It was over? He could go? Suddenly it all seemed so easy and Joey wondered what he'd been frightened of before. "Thank you, sir — Mr. Wynn, I mean."

"Ah." Mr. Wynn smiled slightly. "There's something else, Joey. Now you will call me by a different name, but only when you and I are alone or with team members. Do you understand?"

"I understand."

"From now on you will call me 'Willie Boy.' You needn't ask why."

Joey felt uncomfortable again, but he said, "Yes. Willie Boy. I'll call you that."

"Good. Now one more thing before you go. Your wish."

Joey blinked, not comprehending. "Wish?"

"You get a wish. As you make progress during the season you will be granted other wishes. Today you get one as your reward for making the starting team and signing up. What is it you would most like?"

"I . . . I don't know." Joey tried to think what this man could be talking about. What did he mean, "most like"? Was he about to offer Joey and his family some below-wholesale discounts in the store? "Ah, I guess—"

Mr. Wynn held up his hand. "No. Don't tell me. Wish the way you did when you were a child when you blew out the candles on your birthday cake. You didn't tell anyone, because telling your wish would have broken the spell. Wish in secret for whatever you want the most. Wish now."

He's crazy, Joey thought.

But he made a wish. It was the same wish he made every time he and his family moved to a new place. *This time let Dad be successful in his new job so that Mom won't have to wear old clothes and be ashamed of the furniture when she makes new friends.*

Joey's throat swelled up as he remembered his mother's hurt look each time their new neighbors would come over and see her faded clothes and furniture and then leave without asking her to visit *their* houses. *That's what I wish,* Joey thought.

He took a deep breath and opened his eyes. Mr. Wynn—Willie Boy—was looking at him closely.

His big head nodded. "I understand, Joey. Now go on home and be ready for practice tomorrow morning."

Chapter Five

After supper two nights later, Joey's dad asked him to come into his "office," the small converted pantry next to the kitchen.

Joey was worried. He'd heard his parents arguing the night before and although both of them pretended there was nothing wrong, Joey knew differently. He recognized all the signs: his mother's compressed lips and half-closed eyes, his father's pacing.

Something was wrong again.

So much for Mr. Wynn and his "wish," Joey thought unhappily. No sooner had he made the wish than things had started to go wrong at home; it was practically enough to make a person superstitious. Anyway, hadn't he *felt* that the sporting goods store owner was somehow ... bad luck?

"How'd you like Mr. Wynn?" Frankie had asked him Labor Day night, when the team had appeared in the school auditorium with the cheerleaders for a Parents' Booster Club meeting.

"A weird dude," was all Joey had answered.

"Yeah, but you'll get used to him. It's just the lights and the pictures and all that. Everybody thinks he's weird at first."

"Did he tell you to wish for something?"

Frankie's face clouded over. "Some stuff you just don't talk about," he said stiffly. "That's just the way things are."

But then he'd winked and after the meeting took Joey to his parents' new house and showed him the six-foot video projection screen in his basement game room. *Click,* and there was the Monday night baseball game. *Click,* and now the screen showed a bullring and a matador, his sword held high, taunting a blood-spattered bull. "We're on the sports cable," explained Frankie. "Want to watch him stick the bull?" Joey shook his head no. "Okay, I've got a better idea, anyway," Frankie went on, pulling a cassette from a drawer. "Here's last year's state championship game. We really put it to 'em. Terrific B.C."

"B.C.?" Joey asked.

"Body count," said Frankie with a grin. "The number of injuries the other team gets in a game." During last year's championship game the Norwich starting team had rolled over their opponent by a score of 36-7 on the scoreboard and 0-5 in the injuries column. The zero for Norwich was typical, Frankie told Joey. There were guys on the Norwich team who got the wind knocked out of them or got twisted ankles or dislocated fingers, but not once had an opposing team ever knocked a Norwich starter out of a game; at least not since the first championship season.

Joey frowned. "What about Chris Colman? He told me he broke his leg last year."

"He wasn't a starter last year. Anyway, it wasn't a game when he broke his leg, it was practice." Frankie had smiled. "You just can't believe you got nothing to worry about, right? Well, you'll see. I'm right. It's been this way for seven years," said Frankie, "and it ain't gonna stop, believe me."

Now, as he sat in the rickety vinyl-covered chair across from his father's desk, Joey remembered Frankie's words. *You got nothing to worry about.* Easy for him to say, Joey thought, but if they had to move again, what was the use of being a starter on the Norwich football team?

His father avoided his gaze for a time and concentrated on flaking varnish from the wooden desk top with his fingernail. "Joey," he began finally, "I want to ask you something. Do you know anything about the Clemson-Alabama game?"

"The one this Saturday?" Joey remembered something from the sports page, an article about the Alabama coach. "I don't really know much about it. Didn't they say it's just a warm-up for Alabama? Something about a chance for the defense to start off the season with a shutout? I think that's about it."

His father ran a hand through his hair and stared fixedly at the desk. He seemed to be debating something with himself. "Joey," he went on, "has anyone told you anything about the Clemson team? About what their chances are?"

"No, Pop. Not that I can remember, anyway. Why?"

"Someone told me Clemson was a sure thing; that if I bet on Clemson I couldn't lose. He said to check with you if I didn't believe him, that you'd explain everything. You don't remember?"

"Who told you that?"

"He called himself Willie. He said he was a friend of yours. I met him in a restaurant upstate Monday morning."

"Monday, Labor Day?" It couldn't have been Mr. Wynn, Joey thought. Mr. Wynn had been in Norwich that morning.

"Big guy, dark hair and dark mustache," his father went on. "Wore a brown leather coat. He heard me give my name to the restaurant owner and came up and introduced himself. Said he knew you were a star halfback and wanted to give me a tip."

A cold, uneasy feeling crept into the pit of Joey's stomach. "When did you talk to him on Monday? And where were you?"

"About eleven o'clock, in the Blue Bird

restaurant just north of Humbolt." As he spoke, Joey's father fingered a few papers on his desk and then abruptly picked up the phone book and covered them. He looked up at Joey. "It was my last call of the morning, the farthest north I got. It's about sixty miles north of here on Route Fourteen."

Joey shook his head, trying to understand. "I know a man named Willie who looks like that, but at eleven o'clock on Monday he was here in Norwich, at Wynn's. I know because I was there with him."

"You were at Wynn's Sporting Goods?"

"It was sort of a tour for the guys who made the team. I had my picture taken for the program and got measured for uniforms, stuff like that."

"At eleven o'clock?"

"Well, Mr. Wynn picked me up in front of the school just after ten. By the time he drove to Wynn's and parked and showed me around it must have been at least ten thirty, probably later. There's no way he could have driven sixty miles that quickly and anyway, why would he have gone all the way up there? And how could he have known where you were? *I* didn't even know."

"But did he *say* anything about me when you were at Wynn's? Or anything about Clemson?"

Joey shook his head. "No, he didn't say anything except that you and Mom could get discounts at the store. It must have been somebody else."

"But why would somebody else say he knew you?"

Joey tried to puzzle it out. "Maybe he read about me in the paper and remembered my name." There had been an article about the Norwich team in the sports section of the county paper and Joey had been featured as the high scorer in the final scrimmage at camp. "He was probably from Humbolt," Joey went on. "There's supposed to be a pretty bad rivalry between their team and ours — maybe he wanted to give you a bad tip."

Joey's father rubbed his eyes. "Yeah, I'm beginning to think that's what it was." He shook his head and moved the telephone book to make sure it covered the stack of papers completely. "I guess it was a bum tip, all right."

"Did you bet on Clemson?"

"Don't worry, it was just a small wager." He gave Joey a rueful smile. "And I had such a hunch, too. I really thought it was too much of a coincidence to pass up." Clearing his throat, he stood up. "But there's no good in wailin' over what's past, is there, son?"

A few hours later, Joey awakened. He heard his parents' voices in the bedroom next to his. They were arguing again and it sounded as though his mother was crying. Shivering, he sat up and strained to hear.

His mother's words came faintly through the plaster wall.

"... two months' pay! How you could have ever risked so much ..."

"... don't know what came over me," Joey could hear his father saying. "Until I got out of Oscar's, it was like I was in a dream...."

Oscar's. Everyone knew about Oscar's, even a newcomer like Joey. It was the deli-restaurant in Norwich where all the gambling action went on. Joey drew a deep breath as he realized what his mother had said. Two months' pay! Was that what his father had *bet?*

Then he remembered the papers on his father's desk, the ones now hiding under the telephone book. What were they? Why had his father tried to conceal them? Was there something in those papers that would tell him whether they'd have to move again or not?

Before he knew it he was out of bed and in the hallway. At the head of the stairs he paused, listening to his mother crying behind the closed door of the bedroom. Descending slowly, his bare feet silent on the wooden stairs, Joey hugged the wall, hoping to keep the loose boards from creaking. Still tiptoeing, he entered his father's office and lifted the phone book.

His heart sank as he looked over the papers. They were mimeographed newsletters predicting the outcomes of the upcoming week's football games. Skimming over the first one, Joey noticed that the price for "members" was $75 per week; the price for "others" was $150. Quickly he scanned the other three. Their prices were just as high. Assuming that his father was a member and getting the lowest price, he had still paid a bundle for these papers.

And what had his mother said? Two months' pay?

Finding the predictions for the Clemson-Alabama game, Joey couldn't believe what he read. All four tipsters predicted a "lock," or "sure-thing," bet for an Alabama victory. One of them, the "double-leather" tout sheet, even called the game a "double-lock" in Alabama's favor.

Clemson was going to lose and his father had bet two months' pay. All that money wasted.

Joey suddenly sat up straight in the chair and put down the sheets. How long had this been going on? Could this be the reason why they'd had to move so often? Had his dad's employers found out and fired him? Something told him that gambling was the reason for his father's inability to hold a job. Again in his memory he saw him nervously cover the papers.

"Joey! What are you doing in here?"

Joey looked up sharply, still holding the papers.

"I saw the light on downstairs," his father

continued. "I thought I'd forgotten to turn it off. What are you doing?"

"What am *I* doing?" Hurt and anger surged through him, making his voice crack. Holding up the sheaf of papers, he demanded, "Does Mom know what *you're* doing?"

His father flushed crimson. "Joey, that's not your business! I've tried to get us the kind of things we need, the kind of things I know your mother deserves—"

Joey couldn't bear to listen. Brushing past his father in the doorway, he ran blindly for the stairs.

Locking his door, he sat down on the bed and looked blankly out the window. In the darkened backyard, shirts and trousers still hung on the clothesline. In the dim light of the streetlamp, Joey could see them quivering in the night wind. Shadows from the trees flickered over them, bringing the row of cloth arms and legs to life.

Joey shuddered. What would they do if Pop's money was all gone? Would they stay in Norwich? What would *happen*?

But he couldn't think anymore. All he could do was watch that clothesline and those shadowy arms and legs dancing slowly as though someone had drained them of their last drops of life.

Chapter Six

Mr. Minos was old, but he gave an impression of strength. His bald head a large dome of shiny pink, his fringe of white hair like a kind of wreath, the teacher stood at the blackboard, rapping his chalk for attention. Something about his manner caused the class to come to attention even though some students were still drifting in and looking for seats. In this solid geometry class, he told them, they would study the order that permeates the world and possibly the universe. Did any of them know, he asked, that the knowledge they were going to acquire had once actually been *fought* for? That to acquire it, men had *killed* one another? Mr. Minos gestured at the large globe beside him, speaking in a clear baritone that bore a trace of a European accent.

It was the first day of school. The students listened, already spellbound. The last of the latecomers slipped almost unnoticed into their seats. Joey felt a kind of excitement in the air. This stuff was *real*, he thought, not just some facts he'd need to pass the SAT or get into college. "Geometry was first taught twenty-five centuries ago," Mr. Minos went on. "It was taught in the hills north of Athens in sacred ritual and then in the streets. . . ."

Someone sat down in the seat next to Joey. Glancing over, Joey recognized Bonnie Peterson, the pretty brunette cheerleader he had met the last night of football camp. Their eyes met briefly and then they both turned back to watch as the tall old man, with a bold, sweeping motion, drew what seemed to be a perfect circle on the board.

When the bell rang to signal the end of the period it was as if a spell had been broken. Mr. Minos said anyone who had questions was welcome to ask now or after school. "By the way," he added, "until you get your books, I'd like you to have a look at some puzzles I've made up." He pointed to a stack of ditto sheets on the corner of his desk. "See how many you can do over the weekend."

Students from the front rows gathered around him. Farther back in the classroom, Joey stood up with Bonnie. Her dark eyes were shining. "Have you ever seen anyone like him?" she asked in a hushed voice. "He's terrific! I wish all our teachers were like him." She paused. "I wonder why he's come up here to Norwich, though."

"You mean he's new?" asked Joey.

"I heard he was from New York," someone volunteered from behind them. The class was supposed to have been taught by Mr. Bloom, explained the girl, but he was in the hospital so Mr. Minos had taken over for the semester. "I hope he stays," Bonnie said. Reaching through the crowd around the desk, Joey picked up two ditto sheets and handed one to her. "Thanks. I'm going to work on every one of these," she said determinedly. Joey was about to ask if she had any periods free so they could work on the puzzles together, but then he saw a tall, thin boy with sandy hair and a bright smile waiting outside in the hall. Running up to him, Bonnie took his arm and began talking about what an interesting time she'd had in geometry class.

So that was Steve, Joey thought. Steve the student body president. Joey had noticed his neat button-down shirt, his cable-knit sweater, crisp chino slacks, and shiny loafers. In his blue jeans, sweatshirt, and sneakers, Joey suddenly felt rumpled and unimportant.

Folding the ditto sheet carefully, Joey sighed and put it in his notebook. Monday, he thought. Monday he'd have the whole sheet finished and he'd see Bonnie again. And four days after that would be Friday and

Friday night she'd be out on the football field cheering, saying his name if he scored . . .

What would happen if I asked her out? he wondered. Would she accept? Would she follow the "tradition" that Frankie had told him about? He shook his head. It was foolish to even think about it. If he did ask her out, where would he take her? He didn't have any money and the family car was in the repair shop again —

Joey's thoughts went back to breakfast that morning. Reading the sports pages of the morning newspaper, his father had exclaimed, "They bet *five billion dollars* on the Super Bowl last year!" Glancing up, he'd remembered. "But I've made my last bet," he said, looking Joey in the eye. "There won't be any more." Joey's mother had turned away, crying softly, and then stood up from the table and gone over to his dad and hugged him, saying that if he only meant it this time . . .

Maybe there was hope. Maybe.

But Joey still didn't know what was going to happen, whether they'd be able to stay in Norwich or not. Sure, his dad said he *wanted* to stay, that after Joey had worked so hard at camp and made the team and all they *ought* to stay, but that didn't mean that they *would* stay. Turning this over in his head, Joey was unaware of someone right behind him.

"Yo! Prescott!" It was Frankie. "Whatsa matter, you lost? C'mon, you're gonna be late for practice."

At practice that day the coaches drove them hard. This was their last free Friday; in a week the season would open against Humbolt. "They're always tough," Coach Leach said as they gathered in the end zone for their final calisthenics, "and this year they're going to be even tougher. I want you boys to *concentrate* on what you're doing. I want you to keep your minds on that game. And I want you to keep *each other* aware of our task. Do you read me?"

"Kill Humbolt!" Larry yelled. Soon the others roared in chorus after him, "Kill Humbolt! Kill Humbolt!"

Joey yelled with them. After practice he showered and dressed, feeling bone-weary and not at all talkative. It wasn't the Humbolt game that was on his mind, it was the Clemson game . . .

Beside him, in the carpeted section of the locker room where the senior starters dressed, Frankie and Chris were splashing after-shave on their cheeks and telling Joey about the two majorettes who were their dates for the night. The drive-in, that was the plan.

Chris asked, "We gonna stop at Oscar's first?"

"Sure." Frankie grinned. "Pick up a nice

cold six-pack and say hello to Derrick's old man."

Chris snickered. "Yeah, and ask him if his kid's sent home any paper dolls from the funny farm."

They both laughed. "He won't even notice us," Frankie went on. "Not tonight. He'll be too busy with his marks."

Joey looked up. "Marks? What kind of marks do you get at Oscar's?"

Frankie looked at him pityingly. "What a kid. In town since the summer and he still doesn't know what goes on!"

"What are you talking about?"

"Don't you know what a mark *is*?" asked Frankie, incredulous. "Derrick's pop is the biggest bookie in town. All his action is at Oscar's. The suckers who bet with him are the 'marks.' Now do you get it?"

"I get it," said Joey, trying not to show how sick he felt.

Frankie slapped him on the back. "C'mon, I'll give you a ride home. I've got the old man's Trans-Am."

"No thanks, that's okay," said Joey. "I don't need a ride."

"What, some chick picking you up?" Frankie looked at him with interest.

He shook his head no and nodded toward the second-team section where Andy Blair was shrugging on his army surplus jacket. "I'm walking."

"What, walking home with Andy? Your

good deed for the day?" Frankie shook his head. "For a class halfback, you got a lot to learn, kid." He clapped Joey on the back again. "But you got time. See you tomorrow, hey? And kill Humbolt."

"Right," Joey replied. "Kill Humbolt."

Frankie's basement was a zoo. There were twenty-two guys and Frankie's dad, all crowded into one room, crunching soda cans and yelling as if they were on the sidelines of a real game. Sitting on the thick carpet, Joey watched as Penn State whipped Ohio State on the big screen. Penn ran from the I-formation, the same offense that Norwich used, and Joey could almost imagine that it was he and Frankie up there as halfbacks, cutting into the line and finding daylight. Then came halftime and the "college scoreboard." Flashing a toothpaste grin, the sportscaster announced that in the South, Alabama was leading Clemson by 12-0 in the third quarter.

Joey felt sick. Suddenly it all seemed so meaningless, all of them sitting there in Frankie's game room stuffing themselves with potato chips and pretzels and yelling. It seemed as if all they were doing was making a mess and wasting time.

"I've got to go," he told Frankie, quickly scrambling to his feet. "I promised my dad I'd help him work on the car. See you Monday." He was gone before Frankie could protest, before he could even say "Kill Humbolt."

Outside there was a cold wind that blew away the fumes from the tannery and the paper mill. Joey started to jog. It was about three miles from Frankie's place to his and he was glad for the distance, glad for every inch of it. He wanted to be alone so he could think things through. . . .

His sneakers hit the pavement in a comfortable rhythm and the fresh air felt good against his face. Slowly his mind began to clear.

What's the worst that could happen? he asked himself. *Okay, Clemson loses and we don't have any money. But if it shakes Pop up enough so that he stops gambling, won't it be worth it?* As he ran he felt a little stronger, a little better, as if he'd hit bottom and was coming back up. *After all,* he told himself, *when Clemson loses, things won't be able to get any worse.*

Reaching his own neighborhood, he walked the last two blocks to his house. He didn't want to come in all sweaty and out of breath and he also wanted to be sure the Clemson game was over when he got there. He didn't want to have to watch his father during the last hopeless moments.

The wooden porch steps creaked under his sneakers. As he opened the screen door he heard the radio crackling and the sound of a cheering crowd. " . . . and the MVP for

73

today's game is LeRoy 'Junior' Atkins, a name these South Carolina fans will be hearing a lot of in the coming weeks. . . ."

Joey found his parents in the living room. His mother looked stunned and even a little frightened. His father was unshaven and haggard but his face wore a dazed, relieved smile. For a moment neither of them seemed to have noticed Joey. "What happened?" Joey asked.

"If I'm dreaming don't wake me up," said his father. Finally looking at Joey he added, "Clemson won. I think I've finally learned how to pick 'em."

"Tom, how can you *say* that?" Joey's mother cried.

"Just kidding, Joanie. I won't have time to gamble from now on. I'll be too busy figuring out how to spend all that money!"

Joey barely heard him. In his mind he could hear Mr. Wynn's deep voice saying, "Try to learn something tomorrow." *Is that what I've learned?* Joey asked himself. *That wishes really do come true?* Then he remembered Andy's words. *If you won you wouldn't think gambling was such a big waste.*

"Come on, son! Cheer up!" urged his father. "It's everything we've wished for!"

Chapter Seven

At Oscar's later that afternoon, Joey's dad picked up his winnings from Derrick's father. The two sat at a booth in the back. "Didn't hurt me none," said the fat bookie with a shrug. "Everybody else bet on 'Bama, so I got plenty to cover your winnings. Say, do you want me to reinvest some of the take? A little kiss for Lady Luck, y'might say? I like the Packers for tomorrow and I'm givin' three to one."

"No thanks," said Joey's dad.

"How 'bout the Giants? You're the kind of guy who likes the long odds; I've got 'em eight to one against Dallas. What do you say?"

"Haven't made up my mind on tomorrow yet," said Joey's dad, scooping up his cash. "I'll just take this for now."

"Well, I'll be here till nine." The bookie smiled maliciously.

Joey and his father walked out to the street to where they'd parked the car. Down the block, Joey could see the steel and glass bulk of Wynn's glittering in the late afternoon sun. "Three years," Joey's dad said. "That's how long it would take me to earn what I've got in my pocket. No way am I going to give it back to that old man when I've just — " He looked at Joey. "Do you think I can quit gambling, son?"

Surprised, Joey said, "If you do, Mom and I'll be very happy."

"But do you think I *can*?"

Something in his tone scared Joey. It sounded as if he didn't believe he could do it. Joey didn't know what to say. "Sure, Pop," he managed to get out. "Sure you can. Look at all the other hard things you've done."

His dad exhaled slowly. "But I always had the bet down, do you understand? I always had the hope that I might win. You can't win if you don't play."

"There's other ways to win than gambling, Pop."

"Maybe." He sounded unsure. "By the way," he said, "I stopped in at Wynn's yesterday and had a look at the fella in the leather coat. The one with the mustache. I wanted to see if he was the same guy I met in the restaurant."

"You mean Mr. Wynn?" asked Joey, his throat tightening.

"That's right." Joey's father nodded. "It wasn't him."

It was a coincidence, Joey told himself, or maybe Mr. Wynn had a brother in Humbolt and had phoned him. But still, how would he have known Joey's dad was up there? And how would he have known that Clemson was going to win?

Joey didn't understand.

And on Friday night, when Mr. Wynn came into the locker room at Norwich stadium before the game and told them, "You're champions and you're going to *stay* champions," Joey didn't understand, either. Was there something Mr. Wynn really *knew?* But you couldn't know the future for certain, Joey thought. It was impossible. . . .

"Kill Humbolt!" The cry erupted in the locker room. It was time. Their cleats rattling on the tiles, the team members headed for the tunnel that led to the playing field. Joey was last in line. He felt his stomach tighten and he tasted bile. Just nerves, he told himself, moving to catch up with the others.

At the door to the locker room he felt a light hand touch his arm. He looked up to see Mr. Wynn standing beside him in the shadows. "I know you have doubts, Joey, but put them out of your mind. Your dad was a winner; you will be, too. Remember, your name is in the book." His hand was still resting on Joey's arm. "And remember too, Joey, that you're going to give your best to the team."

Beneath the long, yellowed fingers, Joey's arm began to tingle as if it had been asleep. He felt dizzy. As if from a distance he heard himself say, "My best. Right, Mr. — Willie Boy."

Mr. Wynn looked pleased.

The crowd was screaming because things looked bad. Norwich was one point behind with less than two minutes to go. Humbolt had the ball and Norwich had just called for its last time-out. Standing on the sidelines with the rest of the Norwich offense, Joey watched the defensive players huddle, their red jerseys bright against the emerald-green turf. They looked like they'd been through the wringer, he thought. Humbolt had really come to play this year. Their players far outweighed those on the Norwich team and they had a quarterback who could run the option just as well as Tee Jay, who had brought Norwich back from a 14-0 halftime deficit. Now it was 22-21 and Humbolt had third down and six yards to go on their own thirty-yard line. If they made a first down, on this play or the next, they'd be able to run out the clock for sure and Norwich would have lost its first season opener in seven years.

"They'll take their own sweet time on this one." Frankie's voice was grim. He'd scored one of the team's three touchdowns and

Joey had scored the other two, but neither of them was happy with the way the game was going. "You watch. They'll string out this play as long as they can, maybe even take a delay of the game penalty. They know we don't have any time-outs left —"

"Prescott!" A voice cut through the bedlam. "Prescott!" Joey turned around. Coach Leach, his face beet red, was waving to him. "Prescott, get over here!"

Moments later, Joey was pulling on his helmet and trotting onto the field. "Now in at middle linebacker," boomed the loudspeaker, ". . . number twenty-three, Joey Prescott!" The crowd screamed. They remembered those two touchdowns. They didn't know, though, that Joey hadn't played defense in two years.

"Coach says no changes," Joey told Larry and the other players in the huddle. "I'm just in to key on the quarterback. Everyone else keep doing your thing!"

"You heard the man," said Larry. "Now, do it!" The referee's whistle shrilled. *Whack! Clap!* Fists smacked into palms. "Kill Humbolt!" The huddle broke up. Joey moved to his position, crouched facing the ball, and watched the Humbolt bruisers break from their huddle and line up. He watched the Humbolt quarterback bend over to call the signals and take the snap, he watched the center's fingers close around the ball, watched the knuckles whiten, saw the tendons move.

And then Joey was moving too, sprinting forward as if some sixth sense had told him just when to start, just when the hole between the center and the guard would open up for him to burst through, just which way the quarterback would be running in the backfield. The Humbolt quarterback hadn't taken more than three steps with the ball when Joey hit him, a clean, hard shot around the thighs that took him off his feet. They came down hard, knocking the wind out of Joey. He heard the ref's whistle and the crowd roaring and for a moment he thought the Humbolt quarterback might have fumbled. But that wasn't it; the ball was still clutched in the quarterback's hands. They were screaming for the play to get going again.

Joey stood up unsteadily, his head still ringing from the impact. Fourth down now, he thought, automatically reaching down to give the Humbolt quarterback a hand getting up.

Then he saw the grimace of pain, the eyes rolled back.

He saw the odd angle of the quarterback's leg, saw the trickle of red on the skin below the knee where the sock top had rolled down, and saw the protruding white shard of bone.

He saw the Humbolt coach and managers racing toward him, fear etched onto their faces.

How had it happened? Stunned, Joey bent down again. "Hey, I'm sorry," he said. "I didn't mean—" The fallen quarterback said nothing. His eyes squeezed shut now, he writhed on the ground, moaning softly. There was an officials' time-out on the field while the doctor was called. "Nice hit," said Larry as he and Joey rejoined the defensive huddle. "Bought us some time. They'll have to punt now and we've got a chance." The scoreboard clock was stopped with one minute and twenty-three seconds remaining.

On the sidelines the Norwich band blared the school's fight song. Frankie joined the huddle. "Runback right," he said, "Joey and me deep." There was applause as the Humbolt quarterback was carried off the field on a stretcher.

"You all right?" Frankie asked Joey.

"Yeah, I'm all right." But he kept seeing the red trickle of blood and the white sliver of bone. The ref's whistle blew and the roar of the crowd increased.

Still shaken, moving like a robot, Joey dropped back with Frankie as the Humbolt team lined up in punt formation.

The punt was in the air. A high spiral, a swift-moving shadow against the glaring stadium lights, it was headed for the right side, away from Joey. *A break,* he thought. The runback plan flashed through his mind. Frankie would take the punt and sprint up the right sideline. Joey would block. The idea was to block the opposition to the left and clear a lane. Joey was running now, sprinting across the field, aiming ahead of where the ball would land. *Block left*, he thought, *block left*, and then the first of the onrushing Humbolt linemen was upon him with an impact that slammed them both to the ground. Was it far enough from the sideline to keep the lane clear for Frankie? The Humbolt tackler let loose a string of curses as he watched Frankie sprint past. Then, as Joey rolled to get free, something smashed into his belly. As he went down again he realized that the Humbolt player had deliberately kneed him.

Moments later, still on his knees and gasping, Joey heard the crowd explode in screams and applause. Above the din came the announcer's voice: "Frankie Peters takes it in for the touchdown! A forty-nine-yard runback!"

Chapter Eight

The Norwich team celebrated their victory in the locker room. Coach Leach praised the team's performance "for getting the job done when the chips were on the table." Assistant Coach Gill said the game was "a lesson in not letting the bigger guy intimidate you," and then quieted the cheers only slightly with the announcement that Stockton, the only other serious contender for the state championship, had rolled to a 49-3 win tonight. "You all know what we're up against in November," said Coach Gill. "That last game of the season they'll be comin' down here ready to make us look just as bad as they can, just as bad as we let 'em." He shook a warning finger. "You boys can't afford to get too cocky now."

"Kill Stockton!" yelled Larry.

Joey's stomach churned. In his mind he still saw the Humbolt quarterback on the ground, that jagged bone cutting through the flesh. Cries of "Kill Stockton!" reverberated in his ears and he had to stifle an impulse to bolt from the locker room.

Later, in the shower, he felt worse. Trickles of red seemed to run from the tiles. Sitting on the bench in front of his locker, Joey shivered and drew a towel around his bare shoulders. He felt dizzy. It was that knee in the gut from the punt return, he told himself, that's all.

"Hey, you gonna sit around naked all night?" It was Frankie. "C'mon, get dressed. We got places to go!"

In Frankie's Scrambler on the way to the Victory Dance, Joey still felt rotten. He tried to think about the win and how the crowd had cheered, but he kept thinking about how the Humbolt quarterback must feel now in the hospital, his season ended before it had really begun. Joey couldn't figure it out: how could the kid have broken his leg? Joey had tackled him the right way. . . .

"Too bad about that quarterback," said Frankie.

Joey looked up, surprised. "How'd you know I was thinking about that?"

"Same thing happened to me last year. My first time in on defense I cracked this fullback's collarbone. Guy was their leading rusher and I put him out for the season."

"The first game?"

"Yeah, but you ain't heard it all yet. Couple games later I'm downfield on a pass pattern

84

and they intercept. I make the tackle and the same thing happens. Busted collarbone. I started thinkin' I was some kind of walkin' jinx, you know? Then the fifth game it happens again. Guys started callin' me The Enforcer."

"What did you do?"

"What *could* I do? Felt rotten, that was all. Then I started to make a game out of it, you know, with that body count business I told you about. That made it easier to take, but you never really get used to seein' a guy layin' there. You know the next time it could be you."

Joey nodded. They drove in silence for a time and Joey mulled over what Frankie had said. *This is a first*, he thought. This was the first time that anyone on the starting team had ever talked straight with him about football instead of just going on about honor and dedication to the team. It made things easier knowing he wasn't alone, knowing that somebody else had had the same problem and had come through okay. Joey cleared his throat as they approached the high school gym.

"Frankie?"

"Yo." Frankie turned to look at him.

"Thanks."

He shrugged. " 'S okay. What do you think teammates are for, anyway?" Entering the parking lot, it looked like they were the last to arrive. Frankie cruised around until he found a space and then spun the wheel with the heel of his hand. The Scrambler slipped in neatly between two other cars. Cutting the engine, Frankie turned to Joey. "Now, before we go in and make like heroes, what else is on your mind?" Joey hesitated. "C'mon, I can tell. Somethin' else is bothering you."

Should he say anything? Joey remembered the time when he'd asked Frankie about Mr. Wynn's wishes and Frankie had said there were some things you just don't talk about.

"C'mon, out with it," Frankie urged. "Get it off your chest. Something about the team or what?"

"Not exactly the team —"

"Some chick? That stuck-up Bonnie Peterson givin' you a hard time?"

Joey flushed. "No, nothing like that. She's . . . we just do geometry together, that's all. She's got third period free and so do I."

"Okay, so what's eatin' ya? C'mon, spit it out."

Joey took a deep breath. "Well," he began, "it's Mr. Wynn. He . . . he . . ." Joey didn't know how to go on. He was afraid Frankie would think he was crazy if he told him about the strange feeling the store owner gave him. "What do you think of him?" he asked finally.

Frankie spread his palms and shrugged helplessly. "Who, Willie Boy? Hey, what can I tell you? He's a good guy, knows a lot of people, done a lot for the team."

"But," sputtered Joey, "doesn't it seem odd to you that he *knew* we were going to win tonight? It's like he had it planned. Why would he *tell* us we were going to win?"

"Hey, take it easy. Don't go gettin' superstitious on me now, all right? It's just psychology, that's all. He's psychin' us up! Haven't you ever heard of positive thinking?"

"Positive—"

"Sure. Positive thinking. You think something's gonna happen so it does. Simple as that." Frankie pulled the keys from the ignition, made a fist around them, and gave Joey's shoulder a playful tap. "Don't worry about Willie Boy. He's just an old guy who likes football."

Just an old guy.

Frankie seemed to genuinely believe what he was saying, but Joey couldn't accept it. He wondered if there was anyone to whom he could fully confess his suspicions about Mr. Wynn. There was no way he could tell his parents, he reflected. *They'd probably think I was nuts*, he told himself ruefully. *Maybe I am.*

The night was cooler now. Band music drifted out to the parking lot from the open windows of the school. Looking inside from the car, they could see red and white streamers hung from the high rafters and an occasional couple stopping by the windows for air. A wind sprang up. Suddenly Joey had a prickling sensation in his scalp. He had the feeling that something was waiting for him, that something was watching. . . . Trying to shake away the awful sensation, Joey opened the door and got out of the car. "C'mon, Frankie, let's go inside. We don't want to sit out here all night."

But he wasn't imagining things. As they approached the shadowy area just outside the gym entrance he saw the gleam of smooth brown leather, heard the familiar, resonant voice.

"Good evening, boys," said Mr. Wynn. His face was concealed beneath a wide-brimmed hat. "I'm pleased with you, Frankie. And with you, Joey. I commend you on a fine performance tonight. Both of you have a new wish coming."

Joey didn't make a wish.

He remembered what had happened the last time he'd made one. His father had gotten a tip about the Clemson-Alabama game from a stranger and had put down two months' salary on Clemson, the sure loser. And he'd won. *That's what I wished for,* Joey thought to himself bitterly. *I wished that Pop would be successful and would make a lot of money to get Mom the things she needs. But now,* he wondered, *how's he ever going to quit gambling? Next time he might lose everything.*

So Joey faked it.

After he and Frankie had thanked Mr. Wynn and the sporting goods store owner had walked away into the night, Joey tried to put the whole thing out of his mind. *Blank it out,* he told himself. *Just have a good time.* What the heck, nobody else in Norwich seemed to be bothered by Mr. Wynn. Why should he be the one to act like a scared rabbit?

For a while he succeeded.

Frankie's prediction about the dance had been accurate. People treated the two of them like heroes. Tracy, the talkative blond majorette he'd met the last night of football camp, was the first to congratulate him. Others followed. Soon he loosened up a little and danced, some with Tracy and some with girls he'd hardly even met before.

He was having a good time, dancing with Tracy and listening to her chatter, when he saw a cheerleader with shimmering dark hair swirl past. It was Bonnie Peterson. She was dancing with Steve and they looked like they were having fun together. Joey felt a pang of longing and a twinge of jealousy. Soon he'd have some new clothes, he thought, and maybe his parents would get a new car, and then he'd ask her out. Maybe he'd even ask her to the Homecoming Dance. Perhaps by then she and Steve would have broken up or she'd say yes for some other reason. . . .

He could imagine himself in a new, perfectly cut suit and Bonnie in a white gown, a gardenia corsage on her wrist. . . .

Tracy chattered on. She was *sure* her father would write for the newspaper about Joey's two touchdowns and defensive play, and she knew *all* about the college scouts who were sure to come see the two Norwich halfbacks in action. "Don't I wish," said Joey absently.

Then he realized what he'd done. Panic froze him for a second. Wish? No! He *hadn't* wished for an article in the paper or recognition by college scouts. He wanted to take back the words.

"Are you okay?" Tracy asked, peering at him closely. Sure, he assured her, recovering himself. Just a sore muscle from the game, that was all. Inwardly he berated himself for being so superstitious. As if saying "don't I wish" could really make any difference, he thought to himself disgustedly.

But suddenly he knew what he really wished for. He wished that Bonnie would go to the Homecoming Dance with him.

He wished it. He really did. It wouldn't do any harm to be just a *little* superstitious, he thought. Besides, what could go wrong? Even if the wish came true, it was just a little thing. Just a date for a dance.

Joey sat in the library during third period

with Bonnie. He was trying to concentrate on his geometry homework for Mr. Minos, but he couldn't. It had been almost a week since he'd made his "wish" and he still hadn't gotten up the nerve to ask Bonnie to the dance.

The longer he knew her, the more he liked her. She seemed to like him, too—always asking him about the places he'd lived, about the way the kids there dressed and danced and the kinds of records they listened to. She said she wished she could travel; said that after she graduated she was never coming back to Norwich except maybe to visit her parents at Christmas.

"Did you ever live in a town like Norwich?" she asked, looking up at Joey from the mimeographed puzzle she was working on.

"In a small town? Sure." The Prescotts almost always lived in small towns. You could buy more for your money in a small town, Joey's mother always said. But Joey didn't tell Bonnie that. When she'd asked him why they'd moved around so much, Joey had just said it was because of his dad's work.

"No, I mean a town like *Norwich*," she persisted. "A town where everybody's crazy about football. That's what drives me up the wall around here. Everybody acts like football was the most important thing on earth."

"You and my mom would get along fine," said Joey. "That's what she always says."

"But what do *you* say?" Bonnie looked at him questioningly, her dark eyes serious.

Joey hesitated. What *did* he think of Norwich? "I'm getting more used to it," he stammered. "Pop says it'll help me get a scholarship if I'm on a championship team."

"I wish we had something like the old Olympics," said Bonnie, pointing to Mr. Minos's puzzle sheet. "In the old days the Greek city-states would call off any fights while the games were going on. In Norwich it's more like we're at war with every other town in the state."

Joey was silent. She was right; he could think of nothing to say to defend Norwich.

"Do you know that creepy Mr. Wynn?" Bonnie continued. "Did you hear what he did? Frankie Olivetti asked Harriet to the Homecoming Dance and she said no, because she's already going with Bill Elverson. So when she was in Wynn's yesterday getting a new pair of running shoes, that horrible old man actually told her she should go to the dance with Frankie! Can you believe it?"

"How did Mr. Wynn find out?" Joey leaned forward against the table.

"I don't know. I guess it was gossip or something. But it's none of his business! I mean, it's Harriet's life. It's up to her to decide who she should go out with and who she shouldn't." Bonnie's voice trembled with indignation.

Joey's thoughts raced. So Harriet had said no! She'd turned Frankie down! He wondered: had Bonnie brought up the subject to warn him that he'd better not ask *her* to the Homecoming Dance? Or had she wanted him to be thinking about the dance so that he *would* ask her? Or had she just been upset because of what Mr. Wynn had told Harriet?

Bonnie interrupted his thoughts. "Did you get number five?"

Joey looked at his paper. "He's talking about the Pentagon in Washington," Joey said. "The people who invented geometry in ancient times worshiped the pentagon because ..."

The bell drowned out the rest of the sentence. Joey was about to repeat it, but instead he found himself asking Bonnie if she would go with him to the Homecoming Dance.

Her pretty cheeks flushed slightly. "Thanks, but I ... I already told Steve I'd go with him."

" 'S okay," said Joey. "Just thought I'd ask." He walked her to the library exit, trying not to show how disappointed he was.

So much for tradition, he thought ruefully. *And so much for your "wishes," Mr. Wynn. What're you going to do now?*

He found out the next day. It was Friday afternoon and Joey was the last to finish his physics lab. Leaving the classroom building, he saw four chartered buses lined up outside the high school gym. They were waiting to take the football team, the band, and the cheering section to Monroeville, tonight's opponent. The weekly pep rally had already begun and as Joey crossed the street he could hear the cheers and fight songs coming from the open windows. Entering the old wood-paneled auditorium, Joey found a seat in the back row. The place was mobbed and the rafters shook with the strains of the "Fighting Bulldog March."

Then he saw Bonnie. She was up on the stage behind the lectern, singing into the microphone. She looked nervous. Why was she acting as emcee? Joey wondered. That was the job of the student body president.

But Steve was nowhere to be seen.

"We've got someone missing today," said Bonnie into the microphone. " — Harriet Edelman," she went on. "Our co-captain of the cheerleaders." Bonnie's words tumbled out in a rush. "She had a bad fall down some steps last night and she's in the hospital. The doctor says it's only a mild concussion and she'll be back soon cheering with the rest of us, so let's have a big hand for Harriet, all right? Let's let her hear us all the way across town!"

Joey cheered along with the others.

From where he sat he could see Frankie cheering, too, but was that a smile of satisfaction on Frankie's face?

No, he thought. It couldn't be.

But later, in the cramped visitor's locker room at Monroeville, he sat next to Frankie while they suited up for the game. "Did you get your wish?" he asked, trying to keep his voice light.

"Didn't make no wish," growled Frankie. "I ain't the superstitious type."

Norwich defeated Monroeville 65-3. On the bus ride home, Joey sat next to a very thrilled Andy Blair, who, with the other second-team seniors, had been allowed to play in the last three minutes of the game. Andy had made two tackles. "Two's pretty good for my first game ever," he said modestly. " 'Course it don't compare to your five touchdowns."

"All we needed was one," Joey said, smiling at his friend.

At the Victory Dance the crowd was subdued because the game had been such a walkover. Still, people came up to congratulate Joey on his five touchdowns and Tracy asked him to dance a ladies' choice with her. She talked about how great the game was and how fantastic the Homecoming Weekend was going to be. To Joey it sounded like a not-too-subtle hint. But what the heck, he told himself. Bonnie was going with Steve so he might just as well ask Tracy. "You mean the dance?" he asked.

"Not just the dance," she said, blushing. "The whole weekend. My daddy says all sorts of famous football players are going to be there and you'll get to meet them. And if you're the team's high scorer you'll even get to sit at the head table when they have the big banquet the night before the game. Won't that be exciting?"

Joey was about to reply when a worried voice behind him asked, "May I cut in?"

It was Bonnie. Her eyes were red and her face was drawn and pale. Tracy bowed out gracefully and Bonnie slid somewhat awkwardly into Joey's arms.

She danced without saying a word and the way she moved was stiff and nervous, the same way she'd seemed on the stage that afternoon. "What's wrong?" Joey asked as the dance ended.

She looked up at him as if he'd threatened her with a whip. "Wrong? I ... I just ... could we talk somewhere?"

They went outside. The wind was cold and the air felt raw, as if rain was on the way. Still in her cheerleader's sweater and skirt, Bonnie shivered. Joey put his arm around her, but she shrank away from him. "What's wrong?" he asked, hurt and confused by her actions.

She drew a deep breath. "I want you to

know I really mean this," she said. "I'll go to the Homecoming Dance with you. I'll be your girl, if that's what you want. I'll go to parties with you. Only please don't—"

She faltered.

"Don't what?" Joey asked. "And what are you talking about? I thought you were going to the Homecoming Dance with Steve."

Eyes downcast, she shook her head no. "Steve's gone away," she whispered. "He won't be here for Homecoming."

"You've got to be kidding!" exclaimed Joey. "What is this, some kind of joke? Homecoming isn't till the end of October and that's more than a month from now!"

"He won't be here," she repeated in a louder voice.

"Why not?"

"He's transferring to a private school. Will you go?" She sounded like she was losing her temper.

"Where?" Joey was completely confused.

"To the dance! The Homecoming Dance!"

In the pale light cast by the window, Joey could see that there were tears in her eyes. "Look," he said softly, "it's none of my business, but if you're upset about Steve's going away, why don't you just—"

"Please, I don't want any trouble. Will you just say yes?"

"Trouble? What are you talking about?"

"Will you just say yes? *Please?*"

Suddenly Joey knew what had happened. "Bonnie," he said softly, "has Mr. Wynn said anything to you about this?"

"No!" she cried in a hoarse voice, her eyes wild and frightened. "*No!*" Turning on her heel, she ran back inside.

Somewhere in the darkened parking lot a car engine started. Standing on the sidewalk, Joey stood stock-still, watching the exit to the street. In the pit of his stomach he knew exactly what he was waiting for.

Seconds later, the silver-gray Mercedes pulled out of the parking lot.

"Hey, cool dude," Chris Colman called out as Joey came inside. "Hear you're takin' Bonnie to Homecoming."

Chapter Nine

So my wish came true, Joey thought bitterly to himself. *I should be happy with Steve gone and Bonnie to myself* — But he wasn't. He and Bonnie still met in the library every third period to do homework together and Bonnie went with him to the Victory Dance every Friday night, but she was evasive and difficult to talk to, not the friendly girl he'd known before. No matter how hard he tried, Joey couldn't penetrate the veneer that had settled over her. She was like ice.

She smiled weakly. "Please don't be angry with me, Joey. It's just that I've been so upset."

Joey was silent for a moment. He knew that if he mentioned Mr. Wynn again she would freeze up completely. "Why?" he asked. "Because Steve went away to private school? You must have known that was coming—"

"No!" she cried abruptly. "Please don't ask

me to explain."

"Or is it Harriet?" pressed Joey. "She's still not back in school. Are you worried about her?"

Bonnie shook her head fiercely. "No! Harriet's fine. She'll be back in school any day now, the doctors just want her to get a little more rest."

"Is she out of the hospital?"

"I don't know! Her mother told me yesterday that she'll be back any day now!"

"Then I don't understand why you're so upset!" insisted Joey.

"It doesn't matter!" she cried. "It doesn't matter about me!"

"Who *does* matter, then? What are you trying to say?"

She looked anguished. "I can't tell you, Joey. All I can do is beg you please don't be angry with me. I can't help the way I am. I like you, but I can't help myself."

Wednesday afternoon before practice, Coach Gill gave the team a tongue-lashing. They were all getting fat and lazy, he told them. Their victories of the past month had given them a false sense of security. They were soft and squishy, like fruit, and were ripe for a fall.

So today they were having a live scrimmage to toughen them up.

"And I want to see some hittin' out there!" the coach bellowed. "You hear me? Some *hittin'!* I want to hear those pads and helmets cr-aack!"

In white jerseys, the starting offense went first against the "red" team, the second-string defense. It wasn't much more of a contest than the previous few weeks' games had been. Joey and Frankie ran a couple of sweeps, turning the corner and outsprinting the defenders. Tee Jay, the quarterback, completed a string of passes while Vince, the fullback, ran straight up the middle: once, twice, three times. The third time he broke right through the combined strength of the defense's right guard and right tackle, leaving both linemen flat on the ground.

In the huddle on the next play, Tee Jay called for a 46-counter, a play that required Joey to carry the ball between the two same linemen that Vince had just hit. He got a good jump and slammed through, spun, and saw a clear field ahead to the goal line. A red shirt came at him from the side, but he felt a sudden surge of power and shrugged off the tackle, going into the end zone standing up.

Coming back to the huddle, he saw that the red-shirted player was still on the ground. Suddenly he felt ill. Sprinting over, he knelt down and bit his lip hard as he realized what had happened.

It was Andy. He lay on his back, his eyes squeezed shut in pain. When he heard

Joey's voice, his eyes fluttered open for a second. "It's okay," he said, looking up at Joey. "I think I just dislocated my shoulder."

Mr. Wynn came into the locker room after practice. Andy was in the hospital, he told them, with a broken collarbone and a couple of cracked ribs. There was a chartered bus outside, he continued, and the whole team was going over to the hospital right now to visit him. Were there any questions? His voice took on a slightly menacing tone. Was there anyone who didn't feel he could spare the time?

No one said a word.

"It's a tradition," Chris told Joey as they got on the bus. "Last year the same thing happened to me. I broke my leg just before Homecoming and they all came over to the hospital to see me that same afternoon. You know, to let me know I was still part of the team."

Andy had a private room. It was filled with flowers: daffodils and roses, irises, carnations, begonias, and chrysanthemums, cut flowers and flowers in pots. At the foot of his bed was a large color TV. "He pays for all that, you know," Chris whispered to Joey as they waited in line to see Andy.

"Who?"

"Mr. Wynn. Flowers, TV, the room, everything. Last year my dad didn't have to pay a single penny. The hospital didn't even send him a bill."

Andy's mom, a nurse in the hospital, stood at the side of the bed nearest the door. As the team members filed in, she and Andy greeted them as if they were receiving guests at a wedding.

Andy didn't seem to be in too much pain. It looked like he'd been given a pill or shot that had relaxed the muscles of his face.

Each time he shook somebody's hand he grinned and recited a little speech. " 'S all part of football," he said, slurring his words. "What it's all about is you make sacrifices for the team. Thanks for stoppin' by."

Joey winced. What had happened to Andy? He sounded programmed.

Joey was the last in line. Taking Andy's hand, he turned to Andy's mother, a slender, frail-looking woman in a white nurse's uniform and a starched nurse's cap. "I'm really sorry, Mrs. Blair. I don't know if Andy told you, but I was the one who—"

"It's all right, Joey. Andy's told me. It *is* part of football, you know. We've seen injuries like this in here before. I'm just sorry it had to be you and Andy who collided."

"What it's all about," Andy said groggily. "You make sacrifices for the team—"

"Hey, it's *me!*" said Joey, bending down to his friend. "Don't I get a different speech?"

Andy gave a slack-jawed grin and lay back on the pillow, his eyes glazed. His voice got fainter, as if he were drifting off to sleep.

"You bet. Different. You're different, all right. The new kid. They want the new kid 'cause he's different —"

His mother interrupted. "What are you talking about, Andy?"

He blinked and his eyes focused on Joey. The faraway look was gone now as he raised his head. "Shoulda' seen Joey, Mom. He was awesome out there!"

"I'm sure he was, Andy," said Mrs. Blair soothingly, wiping the corner of her son's mouth.

Joey was about to ask what he meant by that "new kid" stuff but a voice came from the hallway.

"C'mon, Prescott. Bus is ready!"

Joey gave Andy's hand a squeeze. "I guess you better get some rest now. I'll come back tomorrow."

Andy shook his head. "You'll miss the banquet. Gotta say hello to all those pros and college stars for me, Joey!"

"Okay, Saturday morning then. For sure."

Mrs. Blair smiled. The shortest way out, she told Joey, was to turn right and go around to "C" corridor and take the stairs. That way he wouldn't have to wait for the elevator.

Thanking her, Joey left the room and discovered that the others had gone. Rounding the corner to "C" corridor, Joey was startled when a figure in a brown leather coat stepped in front of him.

Joey stopped just short of a collision. Standing outside 14C, another private room, was Mr. Wynn.

Face to face with the man, Joey couldn't help staring at his strangely coarse yellow skin. *It looks like he could shed it,* Joey thought, shuddering as he imagined a glistening thing emerging from underneath. He had a momentary feeling of vertigo, as if he were teetering at the edge of a cliff. "I didn't know you were there," he said awkwardly. "I almost bumped into you."

Mr. Wynn smiled, but his gaze was cold and flat, like a reptile's. "You were going the wrong way," he said. "Come, I'll show you to the elevator."

"Oh, no, that's okay. Mrs. Blair works here. She said the stairs—"

"Come, Joey." Mr. Wynn took him lightly by the elbow and spun him around. "We'll join the others. You don't mind walking with an old man to the elevator, do you?"

In geometry class the next day, Joey was still trying to figure out why Mr. Wynn had been in the "C" corridor. It had to have been for some reason, he thought. Mr. Wynn certainly wouldn't have been just wandering aimlessly around the hospital. . . .

In his mind, Joey replayed their conversation in the elevator. Mr. Wynn had talked about making sacrifices for the team. "It's a shame about Andy," he'd said, "but sometimes, Joey, we even have to hurt our friends. It's all for the good of the team."

His words had chilled Joey, but he couldn't believe that Mr. Wynn would have waited in the corridor just to tell him that.

In the aisle beside Joey's desk, Mr. Minos was passing out quiz sheets. "Take your time," he told the class. "You may leave when you finish or at the closing bell, whichever comes first."

Joey settled down to work, grateful for the quiz to take his mind off Andy's injury and the strange behavior of Mr. Wynn. Geometry was the only place where he could think and come to an answer he *knew* was right. Everything else seemed so murky these days, especially football. It was too easy; he didn't have to try. In geometry he had to work. And in geometry no one got hurt.

When he finished the quiz, he looked up and saw Mr. Minos watching him. As Joey approached the desk to hand in his paper, the old teacher's blue eyes twinkled. "Done already?" he asked, waggling his bushy eyebrows in a Groucho Marx imitation.

Moans went up from around the room. "Don't worry, you all have another fifteen minutes," said Mr. Minos. "Avoid panic and eschew haste. Patience is the beginning of wisdom." Then he added quietly to Joey, "Mr. Prescott, may I have a few moments of your time after class is over? In my office, if it's convenient."

Mr. Minos's office was a small cubicle, undistinguished except for a small bronze statue on the Formica-topped desk. "It's Euclid," said Mr. Minos, "the father of geometry." He reached across a stack of books on the desktop and turned the statuette around to face Joey. "People tell me I resemble him, not that it means anything to anyone. By the way, Joey, you made only one small mistake on your quiz. Very commendable work."

"Thank you, sir."

The old man nodded, then clasped his hands together and leaned forward across the desk to speak. "This might be a bit forward of me, Joey," he began, "but I'm new in town and there's something I don't quite understand. I thought maybe you could help me."

Joey sat back in his chair, relieved to find that he had done well on his test, but puzzled. *How could I help him?* Joey wondered. *And with what?*

" — you're an excellent geometry student," Mr. Minos continued, "yet I've seen you play football and you do very well at that, too."

"Thank you, sir. But why do you say 'yet'?" asked Joey. "The two aren't — " he groped for the right phrase and found it — "mutually exclusive, are they?"

"Of course they aren't, Joey. Or they don't have to be, at any rate. The Greeks believed strongly in the value of sports and they also *invented* geometry as we study it." He paused, and ran a hand lightly over his shiny bald head as if to collect his thoughts. "But here in Norwich," he went on, "sports are a different matter entirely from what the ancients intended them to be. Do you know what I mean, Joey?"

"I guess the town's kind of football crazy," said Joey hesitantly.

"But you're not?" Mr. Minos examined him closely.

"I'm new, you see. I...my parents only moved here this summer."

"Ah." Mr. Minos gave a deep sigh of satisfaction, as though he'd just solved a difficult proof. "That explains it. I thought you had a different look about you." He moved the statue of Euclid aside and took the top book off the stack on his desk. "So we have something in common besides geometry. We're both newcomers. I wonder, have you felt the same way about Norwich as I have? That the town's...a bit out of the ordinary?"

Joey hesitated. "I still feel like kind of an outsider," he said finally.

"I'm not talking about that," Mr. Minos said kindly. "To feel like an outsider in a new town is normal. What I'm talking about is different. Have you ever lived in a town like Norwich where people were so...*intense* about something like a football team? It's as if their whole lives are tied up in—"

"Winning," said Joey.

"Precisely. As long as the Norwich team wins, nothing else matters. And I'm not talking just about the students, I'm talking about the people I see in the stores, in the restaurants, in the faculty lounge, even. Nothing seems to matter but beating another town's children at football each week." His clear blue eyes found Joey's. "I'm telling you this, Joey, because you're on the team and I wondered if you could explain this preoccupation to me. Frankly, I think it's unhealthy."

Joey looked at the floor. He *couldn't* tell Mr. Minos of his suspicions, he thought. It would sound too crazy. Looking up, he said, "I think it's unhealthy, too, Mr. Minos, but I can't help you. I don't understand it myself."

Mr. Minos nodded. "Of course, Joey," he said understandingly. "You're new in town just as I am. It's probably unfair of me to burden you with my impressions, but you're such an intelligent young man and—" He broke off and opened the book he had been holding in his hands. Joey saw that it was a high school yearbook.

"I had a particular reason for asking you to my office," Mr. Minos confessed, thumbing through the book to a page he had marked with a strip of paper. Handing the book to Joey, he said, "I want you to examine this photograph. It's from 1979, the year *before* Norwich won its first state championship."

The picture showed the Norwich High varsity football team. Joey studied the faces. "I don't see anything unusual," he said.

"I don't either," Mr. Minos replied, handing him another book. "Now, take a look at the picture for 1980."

He opened the 1980 book for Joey. There was the team, lined up in jerseys and shoulder pads, holding their helmets.

The difference between the two photos was uncanny. Each of the players in the 1980 picture appeared transfixed by the camera. Their faces were all flat and expressionless. . . .

Mr. Minos pointed to a boy in the front row whose face appeared to stand out from the rest. He was smiling slightly like the others, but there was a lifelike quality to his expression. Joey searched the caption for his name. O'Hara, William. "I'm wondering if he was a good geometry student," Mr. Minos said, winking at Joey. "And if he'd just moved to town."

The old professor slid the stack of yearbooks across the desk. "Here," he said, opening one of them, "look at 1981. There's another young man who appears different from the others. 'Kornfeld, Dennis.' And here's another, in 1982. 'Garrett, Henry.' It's the same for the next four years. In each team photo one face stands out. The rest are blank. I'm wondering why."

"I don't know," Joey said slowly.

"They've made me a faculty adviser to the yearbook," Mr. Minos explained. "That's how I came across all these back volumes." He opened the center drawer of his desk and drew out a slim file folder. "That's also how I came across this nice glossy new photograph."

Joey stared. It was a picture of this year's team taken several weeks earlier by a local photographer. There were Frankie, Chris, Larry, Andy, and the others. They all gazed blankly at the camera as if they were in a trance.

"Which one would you say stands out this year?" Mr. Minos asked.

Joey made no reply. Gently, as though prompting a shy student, Mr. Minos continued. "I know it's difficult to be objective in such matters, Joey, but wouldn't you say it was this young man right here?" He pointed to one of the figures.

Joey swallowed hard and nodded. Mr. Minos was right. One face *did* stand out from the others in this year's team photograph.

Joey's.

That night Norwich held its annual Homecoming football banquet. The high school cafeteria was jammed. Extra tables and chairs had been moved in to accommodate the crowd of starting team members, their fathers, returning starters, and local merchants who were members of the Booster Club. Red and white crepe paper festooned the ceiling and the rows of tables and folding chairs, and the warm smell of fried chicken and mashed potatoes mingled with the smoke of cigars, pipes, and cigarettes.

At the head table were fourteen places. Seated there were four college stars and four pros, powerful-looking men with thick necks and wide shoulders that stretched the fabric of their blazers. One of the college players and one of the pros had graduated from Norwich High during the early championship years. Also at the head table were Coach Leach and Mr. Wynn, Larry and his dad, and Joey and his dad. Larry represented the defensive unit, because he had the most tackles so far this season, and Joey represented the offensive unit, because so far he'd had the highest yardage in total offense.

Seated next to Joey was "Junior" Atkins of Clemson. Earlier, as they had all filed into the cafeteria to take their places, Junior had done something that puzzled Joey. He'd come in just a bit late and gone straight to Mr. Wynn with his hand extended. "Say!" he'd cried. "I didn't know *you* were going to be here, Mr. — "

"Wynn." Dressed in a sleek black tuxedo,

the sporting goods store owner interrupted Junior before he'd been able to finish. "Mr. Wynn," he repeated firmly, as if to make sure there was no misunderstanding. Junior had blinked rapidly and drawn back a little, surprised. Then he'd shaken hands and smiled deferentially, practically bowing to the older man. The other players had done almost the same thing.

Joey couldn't figure it out. Why did these famous people treat Mr. Wynn like such a hotshot? Sure, he was paying for the banquet and their travel expenses, but Joey knew that big-name football players wouldn't be impressed by just plane tickets. . . .

"Had you met Mr. Wynn before?" Joey asked Junior as they ate dinner.

"Naw," he drawled, "but he fooled me. Looks just like a guy I know from back home. In Tougaloo, Mississippi." Junior forked mashed potatoes onto his plate and stole a quick glance at Joey's nametag. "That's where I'm from. You grow up around here, Joey?"

Soon they were discussing the different parts of the country where Joey had lived. As Junior went on about what it was like to be in college at Carolina, Joey overheard his dad talking with a big pro tackle. What were Pittsburgh's chances in the upcoming Monday night game? he was asking him. How about Sunday's matchup between the

Colts and the Redskins?

Joey felt a vague tremor of apprehension. The family had been doing so well, he thought. They hadn't really splurged on anything, but Pop had bought a new car and had gotten Joey his first dress suit ever, the one he was wearing right now and planned to wear to the Homecoming Dance tomorrow night.

"But it's not all football." Junior tapped his fork lightly on his plate for emphasis. "I hit the books on the plane up here and I'm gonna be hittin' 'em on the way back. Got a test tomorrow afternoon and I want to *nail* that guy."

"You came all the way up here for a banquet when you've got a test tomorrow?" Joey asked, surprised.

"We all got to make sacrifices for the team, Joey. That's what football's all about, you know?"

Joey nodded. It was weird hearing one of the leading ground gainers in the NCAA say the very words Andy Blair had mechanically repeated the day before. And what team was Junior talking about? He wasn't on the Norwich team!

Before he even knew what he was thinking he heard himself ask, "Did you sign your name in a book?"

"I sign my name in lotsa books, Joey," said Junior, deftly slicing a piece of chicken with his knife. The look he shot Joey said, Boy, don't you *ever* ask a question like that again.

"Lotsa books," he went on in the same friendly tone. "All the time. People after me to sign my name, seems like."

The book, Joey thought, trying not to be afraid. Mr. Minos didn't know about the book. Joey wanted to tell him.

"Say, Junior." Joey's father leaned across Joey's place to get the Clemson halfback's attention. "Does everyone ask you about that opening game against Alabama? About what you ate for breakfast that morning, that kind of thing?"

Junior broke into a slow grin. "They ask, but I don't have much to tell 'em. I just would get a *surge* out there on the field. Every now and again I'd get one of those surges and I'd just move on out, you know?" He turned to Joey. "You're a good rusher, right, Joey? You ever get one of those surges like I'm talkin' about?"

Joey didn't answer. He was staring at his plate.

Chapter Ten

In the fourth quarter of the Homecoming game, Joey felt another surge. It was almost as if Wednesday's practice had been a dress rehearsal. Running a 46-counter, he hit the line between the guard and the tackle, spun, and saw the goal line forty yards away. His legs seemed to move with a power all their own. The opposing safety came at him from the side and tackled him, but Joey kept right on running, breaking free of the safety's grasp, barely slowing down.

Coming back upfield from the end zone, he'd seen the opposing player still lying on the ground.

They were cheering him, but Joey felt sick. *Why?* he wondered. There was less than five minutes to play on the scoreboard and Norwich was ahead by thirty-five points. What was the *use* of knocking a guy out of the game? He felt as if he was in a dream in which he'd done something awful, only this was no dream. There was the opposing player being carried off the field on a stretcher.

Ever get one of those surges like I'm talkin' about? Junior's voice echoed in his memory. Joey didn't understand. It was as though his mind and body were playing tricks on him. *It's not possible,* he thought. *Nothing can make me run faster out there . . . or make me hurt other players. It's just not possible.*

"Easy," said a voice behind him. "Don't let it throw you." It was Frankie. "Part of football, remember?"

The following night, at the Homecoming Dance, Joey again had the weird feeling that he was living a dream. Here was Bonnie dancing with him, her dark hair flowing, wearing his corsage, dressed in a white gown of satin and chiffon and looking so astonishingly beautiful that he wanted to pick her up and whirl her around. The corsage was of white gardenias, just as he'd imagined it the time he'd seen her at the first Victory Dance. He'd told the florist that he wanted gardenias and had picked out the design himself in the florist's book. He'd *meant* the gardenia corsage to look just the way he'd imagined it back in September. But what made him blink when he arrived at Bonnie's house to pick her up was her gown, her hair. Watching her descend the stairs, he had realized that both were exactly as he'd imagined them in September.

Exactly.

Above the dance floor a shimmering mirrored globe cast dizzying particles of light, like luminous snowflakes, onto the dancers. Finally Joey couldn't contain his curiosity. "Where'd you get your gown?" he asked casually.

"Do you like it?" She sounded surprised.

"Yeah, I do. Where'd you get it?"

She blushed a little. "I didn't think boys were interested in things like that. Dresses and all."

"This one is. Where'd you get it?"

"I—" She hesitated, her eyes darting up to something behind him. Joey felt a tap on his shoulder. It was Bill Elverson, Harriet's boyfriend.

"Excuse me," Bill said. "Do you mind if I cut in for a minute?"

Bowing out graciously, Joey went over to the window to get some air.

When the music ended, Bonnie turned and searched the room for Joey. Spotting him, she rushed toward him, almost running away from Bill as though she was afraid Joey would be jealous. She and Bill had been talking about Harriet, she explained.

"What's the story with her?" Joey asked. "Is she better?"

Bonnie's eyes clouded over. "She wasn't

well enough to come to the dance. Bill is worried. But she'll be fine . . . she just needs some more rest."

Joey could see that distant, wary look coming over her features again. He felt exasperated. "That's what everybody said before," he replied. "But it's been a month, more than a month now, and she still hasn't come back to school. Does she *say* she's feeling okay? Have you talked with her?"

Bonnie bit her lip. "What do you care? You don't even know her."

"Maybe I don't, but I know you and I can tell when you're hiding something—"

She turned away, her shoulders trembling.

"Bonnie," Joey whispered softly, "why don't you tell me what it is? What's the matter?"

"Oh, you don't know," she whispered, shaking her head. "You really don't know."

"Don't know *what?* Come on, Bonnie, tell me!" He was speaking loudly.

"Don't make a scene," she said. "I want to dance."

They moved smoothly into the crowd of gently swirling couples. The music was sensuous and romantic and Joey felt her body press lightly against his. She was right, he thought, cooling down. It would have been stupid of him to make a scene. This was the Homecoming Dance, not some encounter-group session.

He'd asked about her gown, she reminded him after a few minutes of silence. Well, she said, she'd gone to the only boutique in town, the store that Wynn's had bought out last year, and they'd told her they already had this one made up in her size. Since she was going to the dance with a starter on the football team they'd sold it to her for less than half the price.

She gave Joey that glassy smile. "I thought that Mr. Wynn was just awful, but here he actually did something nice for me. So you see, Joey, I've learned something."

He couldn't break through that smile, Joey realized. She didn't *want* him to break through. But suddenly he was fed up. If she wasn't going to tell him what the matter was, he was going to guess. And he knew he was right. "You know, Bonnie," he began, "I don't think you're really afraid of me, I think you're afraid of Mr. Wynn. I think he did something to you and I think he did something to Harriet. That's it, isn't it?" He stared at her, waiting for a response. "Well?"

Her smile didn't change. "He does nice things for people," was all she said.

Joey felt an icy numbness surround his heart.

After school on Friday Joey stopped at Mr. Minos's office cubicle. The old man's eyes twinkled with pleasure as he looked up from his notes and drawings. "Ah, my fellow outsider," he said, beckoning for him to come in. "Did you know they've asked me to design a geometric monument to the football team? I told them it wasn't in my line, but they wouldn't take no for an answer. Would you like to see the sketches?" He slid the papers across the desk toward Joey.

Joey closed the door and sat down. "Actually, Mr. Minos," he said hesitantly, "I wanted to talk to you about something . . .about football, sort of. I wanted to tell you last time we talked, but I was too embarrassed. It sounded too crazy."

"Go ahead, Joey," said the old professor, pushing his spectacles back on his bald head. "Please, tell me."

As Mr. Minos listened, Joey told him of his suspicions about Mr. Wynn, about the "wishes," about the change in Bonnie, and about the strange, hypnotic sensation that had gripped him whenever he'd looked into Mr. Wynn's eyes. "I don't know what to think," he said when he'd finished. "I've never told anyone this before because it sounds so crazy."

Mr. Minos looked concerned. "You mentioned those 'surges' of strength that Junior Atkins was talking about," he said gravely. "Perhaps Mr. Wynn has somehow convinced Junior and the boys on the Norwich team that he is the source of their special power. Wouldn't that be a reason for his having you sign your names in the book?"

Joey wasn't convinced. It was just like Frankie's positive thinking. "Are you just saying that so I won't worry?" Joey asked. "Or do you really believe it?"

Mr. Minos sighed. "I wish I had the answers, Joey, but it's not like geometry where we can apply a theorem to solve a problem. I'm glad, though, that you told me this and I want you to let me know if anything else unusual should happen. And don't worry about sounding crazy," he added with a wink. "You're a perfectly sane young man."

Friday night was the next-to-last game of the season. By the fourth quarter the contest had turned into another walkover for Norwich. In the huddle, Tee Jay called Joey's number for a 46-counter. "Make believe it's Stockton," Tee Jay told him. "Let's see some fire out there. Everybody hits."

But nobody gets hurt, Joey said to himself, his teeth clenched. This time would be different.

He hit the opening in the line, spun away from one tackler, and saw the goal. *Now*, he murmured. *Now*. And sure enough, here came the safety to stop him. This time they wouldn't need any doctors or stretchers to carry the guy off the field, Joey told himself confidently, his legs pumping like pistons, pounding the turf as he poured on the speed. *I'll outrun him, I'll just outrun him.*

He went into the end zone standing up. Untouched.

Turning, he tossed the ball to the referee and looked back upfield.

The safety was lying crumpled on the ground, not moving.

"What happened?" he asked the ref in disbelief. "What *happened*?"

"He made a dive at you; tried for a shoe-string tackle. Guess he landed wrong."

Joey's teammates swarmed around him, pounding his shoulder pads and whooping.

"We're gonna call you The Enforcer yet!" Tee Jay yelled jubilantly.

There were four minutes left to play and the scoreboard read 56-7, Norwich.

From the black sky high above the stadium, the first snowflakes began to fall.

Saturday morning Joey visited Andy in the hospital. His friend was sitting up in bed when he arrived, looking much better and preparing to go home the next day.

"Heard the game on the radio last night," said Andy. "Thought you guys did a super job out there."

"Thanks." Joey smiled and pulled a chair up to Andy's bed.

"I saw Mr. Wynn walk past the room last night before the game," Andy went on. "Was anybody hurt?"

"One of their guys. The safety. No one on our team."

"I don't mean during the game, I mean

before the game," said Andy. "Mr. Wynn walked by just before supper. I was wondering if one of our guys got hurt in practice or slipped in the shower or something."

"Everybody's fine." Joey's voice was tense.

"That's weird," Andy said with a shrug. "Wonder why he was here?"

"I don't know," replied Joey, getting up, "but I'm going to find out."

Leaving Andy's room, Joey rounded the corner toward "C" corridor, half expecting to find Mr. Wynn blocking his path again, but the hallway was empty. And the door to 14C was open. Mr. Wynn had been standing in front of that room the last time.

Inside was a single bed, its aluminum railings drawn up around a patient connected by wires and tubes to a whole array of instruments and bottles. Enough blond hair lay tousled on the pillow for Joey to see that the patient was female. She was sleeping, her head shrouded in bandages, and an oxygen mask covered her mouth.

A chart hung from the foot of the bed. Taking a step into the room, Joey glanced quickly at the name at the top.

His eyes widened and he gasped involuntarily. Checking the name once more, he looked again at the pitiful figure on the bed and then left the hospital as rapidly as possible.

Walking home through the darkening afternoon, Joey was certain that Mr. Wynn was responsible for the safety's injury, too. The store owner had made the hospital arrangements *before* the game. *But how had he known?* Joey asked himself. *How?*

It snowed again that night. Joey had a date with Bonnie. They saw a movie and then went to Oscar's for pizza and Cokes. It was nearly eleven when they arrived, but Derrick's father was still doing business in a booth at the back. Joey took a table on the other side of the room.

"I saw Harriet at the hospital this afternoon," he said offhandedly, watching Bonnie out of the corner of his eye to see her reaction.

She went pale, as if he'd just slapped her.

Joey continued. "Did you know about her all along? That they're giving her oxygen and feeding her intravenously?"

"Please," she said. "Take me home now."

On the way to Bonnie's house she told him. There'd been a car crash. It had happened less than two days after Harriet had broken the "tradition" by turning down Frankie Olivetti for the Homecoming Dance and the very night after Bonnie had told Joey she was going with Steve. "I know it's just a superstition," Bonnie said, "but—"

"I'm not so sure of that," said Joey, looking over at her. "I think Mr. Wynn is behind this. I think he *makes* things happen to people. And I think you know it, too."

She stifled a sob. "Don't get mixed up with them, Joey! Don't go *against* them! You'll get into trouble...." She couldn't continue.

When they reached her driveway, Bonnie flung open the door of the car and jumped out. Before Joey could react, she was at her front door, still crying.

Alone, Joey drove home in the snow.

Frankie phoned him the next day, Sunday afternoon. "Hey, want to make some bucks? I got a few houses to shovel out—split with you sixty-forty!" A few minutes later he came by for Joey in his four-wheel-drive Scrambler. "Got a regular route," he explained. "Some real estate guy, works with my dad's law firm. Got to keep those vacant houses shoveled out regular or you never get back in till Easter."

The third house they worked on was a big stone colonial, its "For Sale" sign nearly buried. "The Wards' place," Frankie said.

"Steve's family? I didn't know they were moving."

"Been gone nearly two months. Ever since ol' Steve got himself arrested."

Joey stopped shoveling. "Arrested?"

"You didn't hear?" said Frankie. "No, I guess you wouldn't have. Family kept it out of the papers."

"You mean he didn't go away to prep school?"

Frankie started to laugh. "Prep school! Yeah, right! Reform school's more like it." He shook his head. "But seriously, don't say anything, okay? My old man handled his bail and got the postponement and all. We don't want anything going around until the trial."

"Trial? Trial for what?" Joey had put down his shovel.

"Promise you won't say anything?"

"Promise."

"Okay, you got to go back a couple months. Our Steve was goin' out with Bonnie. You remember that, right? Well, it looks like Bonnie wasn't enough for Steve. This one Thursday night he went and had himself a little extra date. You remember Harriet?"

The cold was starting to get to Joey. He shivered a little as he nodded.

"Well, Steve's driving her home from the Astro drive-in, arm around her, kissy-face, the whole bit, and when they come around a corner he don't see this little kid out for a moonlight ride on his bike."

"You mean—"

"The little kid's still alive, but just barely. Up to his neck in plaster, you know? But that ain't all. Big shot panics. Out with another guy's girl and now he's creamed this neighbor's kid. He wants to get away before anybody comes out and sees his license number, so he floors it and roars past the next corner where this cop car's parked, and when the cop car comes after him he *really* panics. They figure he was doing over ninety-five when he hit a turn and lost it. Car spins into a telephone pole. Wouldn't you know, the crash comes on Harriet's side. Steve's not hurt, but he's up for hit-and-run and all the rest of it. And Harriet's — " He shook his head sadly. "She had her seat belt on, too. Didn't help her any. From what I hear, she hasn't woken up yet."

Do something! Joey thought. He *had* to do something! But what? He wanted to talk to Mr. Minos, but when he came to geometry class on Monday there was a substitute teacher behind the desk. Mr. Minos was at an important meeting in the Town Hall, the substitute explained. Something to do with the new monument that the town was going to build. Mr. Minos had a very important role to play and the entire mathematics department was proud of what he was doing. . . .

Joey had a vague feeling of apprehension. Was this the way the town was going after Mr. Minos? Getting him on their side by making him a star?

Wasn't that how they got me? Joey thought a little bitterly. All those touchdowns at camp, that ceremony with the blindfold, and then he'd walked just like a lamb into that underground crypt of Mr. Wynn's and signed his name in that book without a single word of protest. . . .

Not even a question. . . .

Class was over, he realized. He'd spent the whole period lost in thought. Bonnie was standing beside his desk.

"What are you thinking?" she asked.

"You don't want to know."

"Oh. That." She turned to walk away, but Joey got to his feet and went after her.

"I understand about what you told me," he said, catching up with her in the hall.

"Will you be quiet?" she snapped.

"Only if you listen to me for two minutes."

He took her elbow and led her to a quiet part of the hallway. "Don't you see," he told her, "that Steve was *made* to take Harriet out? And that Harriet was compelled to go out with him? They were *forced!* Mr. Wynn was trying to punish you and Harriet for refusing to go to the Homecoming Dance with me and Frankie, so he put Harriet in the hospital and he got your boyfriend stuck in jail. And that leaves you . . . and you're going out with me because you're afraid of what will happen if you don't. Isn't that right?"

She was slumped against the lockers, crying softly.

"Hey," Joey whispered, touching her arm, "that's okay. I understand, Bonnie. I'm scared, too. But we have to do something."

She looked up at him, her face streaked with tears. She nodded her head slowly. "You're right," she said in a choked voice, "that's exactly what happened with Steve and Harriet. Even when I was furious with Steve for taking her out I"—she paused for a minute—"I knew that that man . . . that Mr. Wynn was behind it. But what can we do, Joey?" she cried, grabbing his sleeve. "What can we do to fight him? He's not a person . . . he's . . . he's something else." She stared at the floor, her shoulders shaking. "And Joey," she said, raising her eyes to his, "I'm not going out with you only because . . . I mean . . ." She stopped. "I mean, I really do like you."

Joey felt his throat swell. "I really like you too, Bonnie," he said gruffly, "and I didn't ask you out because it's the football player's prerogative, you know."

They looked at each other and smiled and headed back up the hallway.

The next day, Mr. Minos gave a mid-semester test. Joey was nearly finished when he heard Mr. Minos say, "Mr. Frankie Olivetti. Please see me after class in my office."

"Just a little misunderstanding," Frankie told Joey as they walked down the crowded corridor and paused outside the half-open door to Mr. Minos's cubicle. "Wait for me a minute," he said. "I'll be right out."

Mr. Minos's face was gaunt and drawn as he looked up from his desk and noticed them. "Ah, you're together," he said. "Could you wait outside, Joey? I'd like to talk to Frankie alone."

Taking the hint, Joey closed the door and leaned against the wall outside the office. He could hear Frankie talking. "I gotta have a passing grade," he said, "or I can't play in the championship game."

"Nonetheless, you admit you were cheating," replied Mr. Minos. "To ignore it would make a mockery of all that we do here."

"Sir, under the circumstances—"

"I'll have to report it to the principal, Frankie," the teacher said firmly.

"Sir, I wouldn't do that if I were you."

"This is a school, Frankie. A place of education. I have no choice. The team will have to get along without your services."

Moments later, Frankie opened the door and came out.

"Everything's cool," he told Joey. "He ain't gonna do nothing."

They were in the locker room suiting up for practice when they heard the wail of an ambulance siren.

Andy told Joey about it after practice. "I was in the principal's office gettin' my attendance stuff straightened out. You know how you can see through the top of the door to

131

he hallway because it's glass? Well, I just ʌappened to look up and I saw him out here. He looked like he was about to open he door and come in, but then his jaw dropped down and he grabbed at his chest ιnd he fell. I knew right away what had ʌappened 'cause I'd seen my dad when he ʌad his heart attack. I told the secretary, ʌey, you better call the nurse and get an ιmbulance quick. But it was too late. He vas an old guy. Almost seventy."

The funeral was on Thursday morning. Joey skipped school to attend. Only a few ɔeople were there. He recognized the local ɔharmacist and one of the other math eachers, as well as a secretary in the math lepartment. A big, round woman said she vas Mr. Minos's landlady and a wizened lit-le man said he'd been a co-worker of Mr. Minos's in New York. "He has no relatives hat I know of," the little man said, rubbing he gold knob of his walking stick. "And he ɔved these mountains. He used to come up ʌere every summer."

At the snow-covered cemetery on the hill ιbove the town, Joey shook with cold as he istened to the speeches intended to com-ort the bereaved. ". . . loved to show young ninds the eternal truths . . . a full ife . . . working right up to the very end . . ."

What could he do? Joey wanted to tell hese people how Mr. Minos had *really* died, but they'd think he was crazy. None of them would believe him.

He wandered away from the cluster of people at the gravesite. Head downward, he walked with his hands in his pockets, not feeling the snow in his shoes, barely seeing the tombstones that surrounded him. What should he do? The wind on the hillside stung his face. Squinting, he saw the town below: the two small factories with smoke plumes spouting from their tall chimneys, the houses, the school, the hospital, the football stadium. He could see the colorful banners strung across the downtown streets, the blunt, square outline of Wynn's . . . the town looked so peaceful, Joey thought, but he could sense the invisible cloud of evil that hung over it. It was as though Norwich were in a stupor or under the spell of a mass hypnosis.

He pressed on, oblivious to the cold, confused thoughts and fragments of ideas rushing through his head. *What should I do?* he asked himself again and again. *What?*

Without warning, his foot struck something.

Reaching out instinctively to keep from falling, his fingers caught hold of something cold and hard. A tombstone. He'd come to the end of the pathway.

Tired, he leaned against the grave marker, not wanting to move. But he knew he couldn't stay there. He had to get out of the cold.

Turning to walk away, he suddenly noticed the inscription chiseled into the granite.

WILLIAM PAUL O'HARA

1963–1980

OUR BELOVED

"WILLIE BOY"

Joey felt his blood turn to ice. Willie Boy. So that's where he got the name, Joey thought. And William O'Hara was the guy that Mr. Minos had pointed out in the yearbook, the one who was...different.

Then he remembered the geometry teacher pulling out a slim file folder. ..."And I'm different, too," Joey whispered to himself. Suddenly he realized that he was in danger. The last thing Mr. Wynn needed was someone snooping around and raising questions, and after what had happened to Mr. Minos Joey had no doubts about the store owner's powers.

Heading back toward the cemetery gate, Joey knew what he had to do. He had to get the book and destroy it. It was the only way to break the spell that Mr. Wynn had put over the town.

Chapter Eleven

Friday was the day of the championship game. That afternoon there was more snow and the wind blew bitter cold. The streets were already lined with cars, their headlight beams faint behind the falling curtain of white, as Joey's dad drove him to the stadium two hours ahead of game time. "It'll be a packed house," Mr. Prescott said, "but I wonder if this weather's going to break." He clicked on the radio.

The network announcer's voice came on in mid-sentence. "—the stuff that these young champions are made of? Is it hard work, or is it dreams, or is it more than that? Is it an elusive 'something' that strikes only a few of us once in a great while, something that's beyond our capacity to understand even when it's right before our eyes? Maybe so. But whatever it is, it makes our hearts beat a little faster and with a little more pride.

"And so," he continued, "on this November Friday night, as the longest high school winning streak in the nation goes on the line way up there in Norwich, we salute you young men and wish you well. May the best team win. And now, please, this message."

"Oh, my," Joey's dad said softly. "Oh, my."

The first half ended with a tie, 7-7. During the halftime break, the Norwich team hunched on their benches in the locker room, trying to warm their frozen hands and feet. Coach Leach stood before them, hands in his pockets, head bowed. He asked them to think back to those mornings in camp when they'd gone splashing into that cold river water, back to when they'd run those extra miles and taken those extra hits, back to when they'd pulled the Humbolt game out of the fire. "All for one thing, boys," he said. "All to prepare you for this moment."

"Kill Stockton!" yelled Larry.

The locker room resounded with the cry.

As the team headed back down the tunnel for the second half of the game, Joey stepped aside. "Gotta hoist," he told Frankie. "Be right out." Ducking into the toilet, he closed the door.

When the last echo of cleated footsteps had faded away, Joey ventured a look.

The locker room was deserted.

Quickly he kicked off his cleats, wriggled out of his jersey and pads, rolled them into a ball, and stuffed them, with his helmet and varsity jacket, as far down into a trash barrel as they would go. Then he covered them with newspaper. Hurrying, he pulled on his school clothes, his sneakers, and his old green hunting jacket.

Thirty minutes of playing time. With the weather and more incompleted passes and time-outs there was maybe an hour of real time left. Wynn's Sporting Goods was a five-minute run from the stadium; Joey had timed it the day before.

Turning up his jacket collar, Joey left the locker room by the rear entrance, heading back through the central corridor. It was filled with the Stockton players in their blue uniforms, stamping their cleats on the floor and clapping their hands together, getting psyched before they hit the tunnel and made the dash into the arena. Joey burrowed his chin into his coat as he edged past; no one recognized him. At the refreshment stand, people were clamoring for the attendants to hurry up with their hot dogs and coffee. Joey kept his head down as he passed through and stayed that way as he passed the security guards at the ticket lanes. "Got your stub, son?" a guard called after him. "Can't get back in without your stub!" Joey held up a closed hand and waved it as if he was holding a ticket.

Now was the only time, he knew. The only chance he'd have to get to the book was during the championship game when Wynn's was closed up, when everyone was concentrating on the events at the stadium. If he didn't take it now it would be gone forever.

Soon he was in the narrow alley outside the rear entrance of Wynn's, squinting up through the falling snow at the fire escape that led to the third floor. He faltered. He had been so certain about coming here. Now he was afraid. What if he got caught? But he had to get that book. He jumped for the bottom rung of the fire escape. Once. Twice. He'd just get his fingertips around it and then they'd slip off.

Then he noticed some trash cans from the restaurant across the alley. His hands rapidly numbing from the cold, he maneuvered one of them into place beneath the fire escape and climbed up. Jumping, he caught the bottom rung and held on.

The rubber soles of his sneakers slipped on the icy metal as he climbed, but he clung determinedly. Moments later he was at the top of the fire escape, standing on the metal grid, looking through the wire-mesh glass window of the fire door and trying to catch his breath. Lights were on at the office level. *Odd,* Joey said to himself, *I'd have thought that everyone would be at the game.*

He could see a white corridor and white doors. One of them was partially open and he could see lights on in the office inside, too. On the other side of the hallway was an elevator.

Practically covered by the snow, embedded in the wall on the right side of the fire door, was a small panel with ten numbered buttons: it had to be a lock mechanism.

Taking a deep breath, Joey pushed the buttons in the same sequence he'd seen Mr. Wynn use on the computer terminal the day of Joey's "initiation." Then he tried the latch.

The door opened.

He was inside. No alarm bells were ringing. Carefully, Joey closed the door behind him.

His wet sneakers were slippery on the tiled floor. Moving as silently as he could, he kept close to the wall, making for the elevator. As he passed the open office door he heard voices. Someone *was* up here! His heart pounded as he looked over his shoulder. He'd have to take the elevator down to the storage room before anyone realized he had broken in. Then if he could use the same number code on that computer terminal to open that vault—

If!

A man's voice from inside the office said, "Turn it up, why don't you?" Joey heard a radio sports announcer. "Fourth and four for Norwich—" They were listening to the game.

He pressed the elevator button.

Nothing happened. No machinery hummed. The light didn't go on. He pressed the button again. Still nothing.

Cold perspiration broke out on his forehead. Were there stairs? Checking the hallway, all Joey found was a men's room and a ladies' room and those other doors. He opened each of them a crack, holding his ear to the metal cladding and listening. At each door he heard the same thing: voices and the radio announcer. The doors all led to the same room. There were no stairs; the elevator was the only way down.

To his left, voices suddenly grew louder. "Be right back!" someone called. Joey's heart hammered loudly in his ears. Someone was coming! It was too late to run for either of the rest rooms.

No choice, he thought, ducking into the office through the door on his right.

He found himself between two opaque glass partitions in a kind of miniature hallway that separated two work cubicles. He crouched behind one and looked around. The office was brightly lit. He could see five men bent over computer terminals. But all the other terminals were lit up too, glowing with what looked, from a distance, to be names and numbers.

Joey peered into the nearest cubicle. At

the top of the computer screen he saw:

SUNDAY, NOV. 14. DALLAS — GREEN BAY
1. NICHOLS returns   2. MARCUS pass
   CZACK'S kickoff   to WOLTMAN
   D4 — D36   D36 — D45

Joey stared at the rest of the play-by-play description, astonished. The neatly numbered column extended all the way down to the bottom of the screen.

They had the game all planned. The whole summary was right there on the computer screen. Every play and every result.

And November 14 was two days from now —

The radio announcer's voice crackled. "Eight minutes remain in the third quarter. Norwich first and ten on their own forty. Olivetti and Barton the halfbacks — "

One of the computer operators looked up. "Hey, isn't Prescott still the other halfback?"

"Who knows?" said another. "The boss did the numbers for this one. Maybe they're resting him."

"I saw a chart," a third said. "Eleven minutes into the fourth quarter Prescott takes a pass in from the Norwich thirty-one. Breaks it open."

"That's strange," said a fourth voice. "Wonder what happened?"

Crouched behind the partition, Joey felt that his mind had slipped beyond the bounds of reality and had entered a twilight, nightmare world. It wasn't possible, he frantically tried to tell himself. No one could make people do things, no one . . .

Suddenly Joey was aware of an alien presence. Something was with him, standing over him.

Before he could move he felt it strike like a cobra. Something hot and sharp was digging underneath his jacket collar, burrowing down so quickly that he couldn't begin to fight it. He couldn't move.

Slowly the long fingers manipulated his neck, turning his head around. Joey felt hot breath scald his cheeks, saw the rough, yellowed skin. Against his will he lifted his gaze to meet the yawning black eyes of Mr. Wynn and he stared directly into the abyss.

"Made a mistake, didn't you, Joey?" crooned the familiar voice.

Coming to slowly, Joey struggled to make out where he was. Little by little he discerned the X-ray equipment of the "initiation" room. He was stretched out on his back, his limbs pinned to the steel table by an invisible force. He tried to move but could not.

Then he saw Mr. Wynn standing beside him, a slim blade glittering in his hand. His breath was warm and putrid, his face twisted in gleeful triumph. Joey thought of roaches and beetles and how they break out of their larval coating when fully formed. It seemed as if Mr. Wynn's yellow skin was only a brittle covering, a mask that would break to reveal the dark thing inside.

The man chuckled softly. "We've all got to make sacrifices, Joey. For the team."

Joey trembled inside, but he was determined not to show his fear. "I saw the tombstone," he said finally.

"Did you, indeed? What did you conclude, Joey?"

"Now I know why you wanted us to call you Willie Boy." He drew a deep breath and went on. "It gives you a thrill, doesn't it? Hearing kids say his name when they don't know he's dead?"

"He was my first," Mr. Wynn said reflectively. "Young O'Hara. A fine wide receiver, but curious. Curious like you, Joey."

"What about the others?" Joey persisted. "What about Dennis Kornfeld and Henry Garrett? Weren't they curious, too?"

Mr. Wynn chuckled again. "You *have* been diligent, haven't you, Joey? But I guess that geometry teacher of yours was a help." He smoothed his mustache with a long finger. "I don't suppose it would hurt to tell you, since you'll never be able to talk about it. . . ."

Joey felt his heart contract in terror, but he struggled to remain outwardly calm. *I've got to keep my wits about me,* he told himself fiercely. *I've got to think.*

"You see, Joey," Mr. Wynn began, "I'm part of a large organization that specializes in the transfer of energy. Now perhaps you'll understand all those injuries on the field and those surges of strength you got. Or do you still think those were accidents or just the result of good training?" He threw his head back and laughed, a raw, hideous sound. "You have to take from one to give to another, Joey," he said. "There is only limited energy and to give to one you must sacrifice another. You have to remember that.

"My personal interest is young people," he went on, "which is why I concern myself with your football team. I chose Norwich because of its unobtrusive location and because of its climate. You see, Joey, I need the cold to keep me healthy."

"Embalmed," Joey corrected bitterly, eyeing the blade in Mr. Wynn's hand.

"If you prefer," the man replied simply. "Had you gone on for a career in football you would undoubtedly have met some of my associates. A pity you won't have that opportunity." He cackled maliciously. "Today we control what you might call the 'darker' side of sports," he continued. "We traffic in human vulnerability. We tempt people, we lure them into our net so we have them when we need energy for a project. You have to understand, Joey," he said, tracing the knife lightly over Joey's chest, "that our goal is to have complete mastery of the human race. We'll control the world."

"You're like a vampire," Joey said, trying to keep his voice from breaking. "You feed on other people's lives, on other people's weaknesses. You're a parasite, a bloodsucker—"

"Nothing comes free in this world, Joey, but people refuse to admit it; there's always a trade-off. That's another reason why I chose to do my work in Norwich. I saw a town that was without inspiration, a poor town. I saw that the people here would put aside their good sense—their values—for recognition. I tempted them, Joey, and I won. I won!"

"What are you going to do?" Joey asked suddenly.

"In a few minutes the game will be nearly over. Young Frankie will be tired, he'll need a surge. You'll provide it."

Revulsion and horror filled Joey, and his eyes were fixed on that gleaming knife.

"You're going to give your best to the team, Joey," the man whispered, his hot fingers stroking Joey's cheek. "By the way, I may save your little Bonnie and her two friends, Harriet and Steve. After all, she says I do nice things for people."

"Does it make you feel powerful—"

"Which one would you choose?" the store owner broke in. "I had prepared all three for tonight, you know."

"Leave them alone!" Joey yelled. "They've suffered enough!"

Mr. Wynn clucked his tongue. "Always thinking of others. That's been your problem all along. I knew from the start that I couldn't buy you off with television sets or electronic games. No, you were different." He sighed. "But now I have to leave you for a few minutes," he said calmly, punching a code into a numbered panel that opened the wall. "I must go upstairs to prepare the game for what will be Frankie's moment of triumph. Your absence has made a shambles of the entire third quarter." The wall slid shut behind him with a click.

Alone, Joey found that he could move his arms and legs. They tingled painfully as if the circulation had been cut off for a long time. *Come on, move!* He knew he had to escape. But how? Gingerly climbing down from the table, Joey hobbled over to the numbered panel on the wall. *Here goes nothing,* he thought grimly, punching in the code that he'd seen Mr. Wynn use that first day, the same code that had opened the emergency door upstairs. To his amazement, it worked. The wall slid open. Ignoring the pain in his legs, Joey rushed to the table and yanked open the drawer. The book was there. Lifting the heavy volume, he hugged it to his chest and sprinted through the door into the stockroom. But now what? The big garage doors at the loading bay were controlled by the computer and there was no way he could take the elevator upstairs...

Seating himself at the computer terminal, Joey found the "on" button and pushed it in. The screen stayed blank, but from the electric innards of the machine came a soft hum. Carefully he pressed the numbered buttons in the same coded sequence that he'd used earlier.

7-7-3-4.

The wall to the altar room slid open again, but the garage doors didn't budge. He should have known it wouldn't be as easy as all that. Mr. Wynn would never be that careless.

Abruptly his gaze fell on a shelf close to him. Reaching up, he pulled down two clear plastic bags and tore them open. Inside were thick red and black wires with copper, jawlike clamps.

Moments later he had pulled down two 12-volt DC storage batteries from the top shelf and lugged them over to the computer. *At least I'll give him something to remember me by,* he thought grimly.

Working as fast as he could, he clamped both sets of the jumper cables to the positive and negative poles of each battery and then attached one set of clamps to the connecting wires at the back of the terminal.

Then he took a deep breath. *Here we go,* he thought, attaching the third clamp to one of the first two, red to black, minus to plus. Gritting his teeth, Joey wrapped the plastic bags around his hand to insulate it as he picked up the last unconnected clamp.

Black to red. Positive to negative. It would be a short circuit as soon as he clamped it...

On!

The jolt knocked Joey's hand away and flung him to the floor. But the clamp held! He could see the wires starting to glow red-hot as the electron juices flowed between the two batteries and through the computer. The screen was no longer blank but a scrambled maze of symbols, as though each little microdot was being switched on and off in every available combination—

The sudden wail of a siren made Joey freeze. He'd tripped an alarm; Mr. Wynn would be down there in no time—

Just then the doors to the loading bay started to rumble open. There was a space big enough to crawl through and Joey could see the snow falling outside.

Quickly he backed away from the computer. It was glowing red now and acrid fumes began to pour from the interior connections. Choking, Joey realized that the insides of the machine were now no more than molten metal and burning sludge.

"Give me that book!" The voice cut through the smoke like a knife. "DROP IT!"

By the glowing light of the ruined terminal, Joey could see Mr. Wynn approaching, the knife gripped in his raised hand. *Don't look at his eyes,* Joey told himself fiercely. *Don't look!* One look at those eyes, Joey knew, and he'd be paralyzed, he would be under the spell.

His head down, Joey held out the book toward Mr. Wynn. The man inched closer, trying to stay away from the red-hot computer. The heat was intense and sweat poured down Joey's face, but he kept the book in front of him.

"That's it, Joey," the man crooned, "just give me the book. You pledged to give your best to the team. You wouldn't want to break that promise now, would you?" His voice was coaxing, as if he were talking to a recalcitrant child.

Then, just as the long, talonlike fingers touched the leather binding, Joey heaved the book up and forward, sending it crashing into the fiery computer.

A fireball rose to the ceiling with a roar. Joey lunged behind a shelf for protection and watched, horror-stricken, as the blaze engulfed the thing that had called itself Mr. Wynn. A howl escaped the man's throat as the dancing flames consumed his dried, yellow skin. Within minutes all that remained of him was a foul-smelling black liquid that drooled out of his crumpled clothing.

Retching and gagging, Joey stumbled toward the partially opened loading doors. He hit the concrete in a rolling dive and found himself over the edge, falling. . . .

He landed on his side in the snow beneath the loading dock, his arm twisted under him at an awkward angle. He could feel the first awakenings of pain, but he didn't care. Norwich was free.

Joey entered the library as the bell signaling the beginning of third period sounded. Looking around, he spotted Bonnie at a table by the window. She saw him and smiled.

"How does it feel?" she asked him, looking at his arm in its sling. "Does it hurt?" She touched it gently.

"No," said Joey, sitting down, his eyes on her concerned face. "Just a little break. It's okay."

"I saw Derrick today," she said. "He's back at school. It seems he has no memory of what happened, thinks he was just sick for a while."

"That's for the best," Joey replied. "After the way Mr. Wynn used him to do his dirty work it's just as well that he forget the whole episode. I think we all should."

Bonnie nodded her head in agreement. "It'll take a while, though. I mean, the police are still trying to figure out what happened."

Joey shrugged. "They'd never believe the truth. But I guess little by little the mystery will be forgotten." And then he added, "Thank goodness."

There was a pause. "You know, Joey," Bonnie began slowly, "I want to thank you for what you've done. It's like Norwich has come back to life again...I can feel it."

Joey didn't know what to say. "I know," he murmured. "I can feel it, too. I think this town will be a good place to be. And things are working for my parents, too. My dad's finally settling into his job, and Mom... well, she's happier than she's been in ages."

Bonnie nodded, blushing a little. "Harriet's home," she said, looking up at Joey. "She's feeling a lot better. She should be back at school next week." Seeing Joey's dubious look, she added, "This time for sure."

But there was something else Joey wanted to know. "What about Steve?" he asked. "What happened to him?"

"His family decided to leave Norwich for a while," Bonnie explained. "After all that's happened, I guess I can't blame them."

Bonnie and Joey looked at each other for a moment in silence.

"Hey," she said softly, "do we still have a date for Friday?"

Joey smiled and reached across the table for her hand. "You bet," he said, squeezing it. "You bet!"